She wa[...]

'As I tho[...]'t a
thought for[...]her
head in dis[...]made a bad
character ju[...]. For one atom of a
second I liked you; even knowing what I knew
about you, I was prepared to give you the
benefit of the doubt. But there isn't any doubt
now. You can't even deny it!'

Dear Reader,

In February, we celebrate one of the most romantic times of the year—St Valentine's Day, when messages of true love are exchanged. At Mills & Boon we feel that our novels carry the Valentine spirit on throughout the year and we hope that readers agree. Dipping into the pages of our books will give you a taste of true romance every month...so chase away those winter blues and look forward to spring with Mills & Boon!

Till next month,

The Editor

Natalie Fox was born and brought up in London and has a daughter, two sons and two grandchildren. Her husband, Ian, is a retired advertising executive, and they now live in a tiny Welsh village. Natalie is passionate about her two cats, two of them strays brought back from Spain where she lived for five years, and equally passionate about gardening and writing romance. Natalie says she took up writing because she absolutely *hates* going out to work!

Recent titles by the same author:

LOVE ON LOAN
A LOVE LIKE THAT
LOVE OR NOTHING

POSSESSED
BY LOVE

BY

NATALIE FOX

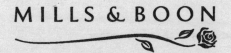

MILLS & BOON LIMITED
ETON HOUSE, 18-24 PARADISE ROAD
RICHMOND, SURREY TW9 1SR

*First published in Great Britain 1993
by Mills & Boon Limited*

© Natalie Fox 1993

*Australian copyright 1993
Philippine copyright 1994
This edition 1994*

ISBN 0 263 78398 7

*Set in Times Roman 10 on 12 pt.
01-9402-51886 C*

Made and printed in Great Britain

CHAPTER ONE

'I DON'T need this!' Fern seethed into the chill night air, her teeth chattering. She crammed her long auburn hair under her woolly scarf and stood muffled against the sharp wind, letting her eyes accustom to the dark. As if she hadn't enough to contend with. After today she was a town girl after all, she decided.

Suddenly the moon broke through the clouds and Fern could see the dilapidated log barn clearly. There was a break in the wire fence next to it; she'd seen it in daylight and thought at the time it was just the place for a scatty golden Labrador to abscond through. Fern ran towards it and stepped into the frosty meadow beyond, put her finger to her mouth, and whistled shrilly.

A monster suddenly reared to her left and Fern's scream of terror soared into the air in hot pursuit of her whistle. There was a snort of fiery hot breath, an inhuman whinny, the sudden crack of thrashing hoofs on frozen mud, then an earth-stopping muffled thud, and finally a very human snort of rage.

Oh, my God, a horse! Fern ducked. It was almost on top of her!

'Grab the reins, for God's sake!'

'Reins!' Fern squawked. Desperately she looked to see where the voice was coming from, but the monster of a horse was about to rear up again. Something leathery slapped against the side of her face and she snatched at it. She hung on and tugged fiercely.

5

'Easy, girl! Easy, girl!' she soothed, so terrified that she was in need of some soothing herself.

'*Boy!*' scathed the voice from somewhere around ground level. 'Don't you know the difference between a stallion and a mare?'

The ridiculous question was almost as ridiculous as what Fern was doing now—running her hand down the nose of the first horse in the world she had ever intimately swapped breath with. She gathered the loose reins around her hand to keep a grip on her—him!

'In the dark I wouldn't know the difference between Donald Duck and Dumbo!' Fern retorted breathlessly as she held on to the spooked horse for grim death. 'Are you all right?' she asked, peering around her. The moon had long since gone and the darkness was impenetrable.

'Yes, but no thanks to you and that ear-piercing whistle.'

Suddenly there was another presence next to her—a tall, puffing human figure, which, though faceless in the gloom, was a male by voice and fury.

'Sorry, but I was hardly to know you'd be galloping around the countryside like one of the last horsemen of the Apocalypse!'

'And I was hardly to anticipate a raving banshee screaming in the night. What the devil were you doing anyway?'

'Only whistling my dog, not summoning the spirits of evil,' Fern retaliated crisply. 'I don't suppose you've seen her on your ghostly travels?'

'A crazy flea-bitten golden Labrador?'

'She is *not* flea-bitten!' Fern insisted, smarting with the insult for her son's dog. 'She's just a little distressed-looking. She was rescued from an unloving home and has spent the last few weeks in a dogs' home, and you've obviously seen her, in daylight, so which way did she go?'

'Straight into one of my barns, and that's where she is going to stay for the night. She's confiscated.' His voice was so loaded with contempt that Fern hoped his backside stung from his unceremonious dismounting.

'What do you mean—"confiscated"?' She spluttered in disbelief, imagining herself having to do five hundred lines to secure Sacha's freedom. 'You can't confiscate a dog; it's a being, not a pea-shooter.'

She was aware of the dismounted rider cum Dickensian schoolmaster furiously brushing the seat of his trousers. She wished he'd hurry up and sort himself out; the reins were cutting into her fingers.

'She was in my yard, yapping at my sheep, so I locked her up——'

'You can't do that!'

'I already have.' He fumbled to unwind the reins from her half-frozen fingers.

'Hang on! Patience, patience,' she cried, shaking her hand to be free.

'Well, patience is something I'm very short of today. I've been chasing that stupid bitch——'

'Sacha *isn't* a bitch! Don't you be so damned rude!'

'Bitch as opposed to dog,' the rider huffed impatiently.

'Oh, yes, of course,' Fern mumbled, plunging her frozen hands into her pockets for warmth. 'Anyway, you can't lock her up.'

'It's done. That'll teach her a lesson. She's been rampaging around the yard and the stables all night——'

'She hasn't been out *all* night,' Fern protested. Charley would go mad if he didn't find her curled at the foot of his bed when he awoke in the morning. 'She'll freeze in a barn. Just you let her out or else.'

'Or else what?' The voice was so derisive that Fern wanted to slap him, whoever he was. 'I could have shot her instead of putting her up for the night, so don't you forget it. And she won't freeze in a warm hay barn and she won't go hungry either; my daughter insisted on feeding her.'

'Oh,' Fern let out ineffectually. 'Well, I suppose I ought to be grateful for you having at least one humane being in your household. By your attitude I gather *you* would rather have opted for the firing-squad!'

There was a small silence in which Fern weighed up the thought that he must own the land that surrounded her cottage; that he was some ruddy-faced farmer with more clout in these parts than the bankers and money-market moguls who took up residence in this green-belt area of Surrey. Trust her to bump into one on her first night here.

Suddenly she heard the muted rustle of oiled cloth, then a torch shone out brightly and Fern blinked and turned her face away.

'Who the devil are you, anyway?' the horseman grated.

Her arm across her eyes, Fern spoke icily. 'Fern McKay. I've just moved into Meadow View Cottage. Now will you lower that light so I can see my inquisitor?'

The beam of light shifted to the frosty ground they were standing on, and slowly Fern raised her head to look at him.

Her gasped shock of recognition was obliterated by the sudden impatient snort of the stallion standing next to her. Instinctively she took a step back, not in shock but in disgust. His looks were certainly not disgusting and he could hardly be described as a ruddy-faced farmer. No, his looks were clean-cut, sharply good-looking, and he was the last person on earth she'd expected to come face to face with. Her disgust was inevitable because he'd mentioned a daughter and that meant he was a married man.

'So, Kay McFern,' he drawled. 'I won't welcome you to our community, because you and your dog aren't. I have valuable stock here and your dog is a nuisance, and I have a feeling you will be too.'

Fern took another step back. She cared nothing for his insults now or his abrasive manner, but adulterous men were another thing altogether. This man towering over her with his wretched horse snorting impatiently over his shoulder was having an affair with Rachel Edwards. Perhaps she shouldn't be shocked by that. Rachel, the rich, spoilt daughter of her brother Tim's business partner, had an avaricious appetite for men. She had even made a play for Tim once, but Tim was made of sterner stuff. A confirmed bachelor by nature, he had resisted, and now apparently Rachel was heavily involved with this…this married man. No, she shouldn't be shocked; they looked as if they deserved each other. She suppressed a shudder, turning it into a shiver of cold, because it was none of her business. But a man who played away from home was a creep in Fern's eyes, especially when there were children involved.

Suddenly he tugged at the reins and turned his stallion so that he could leap into the saddle. He paused before digging in his heels. 'If you want your bitch back you'd better be up at Bourne Hall to collect her first thing in the morning. If you're not there by ten she goes back to where she came from—the dogs' home!'

His heels went in and the stallion shot forward and was in full gallop across the field before Fern found her breath and shouted after him, 'If any harm comes to Sacha you'll be the one in the doghouse!'

She was numb with cold and shock by the time she was back in the cottage. Standing in front of the Aga in the kitchen, she slid out of her oiled jacket and warmed her hands.

There was no sound from upstairs. Charley had fallen into bed after their first hectic day in the new house, so exhausted that he hadn't noticed Sacha hadn't returned. She would have some explaining to do to her six-year-old the next morning.

Fern made herself a cup of tea and stared bleakly at the stacks of boxes and cartons yet to be unpacked, but it was impossible to work, because that arrogant man had upset her. Damn him; he was her closest neighbour, and what a way to meet for the first time! And it didn't help knowing what she knew—that he was romantically involved with the beautiful Rachel. His wife was her neighbour as well and could be a lot friendlier than her beastly husband. She might suggest a coffee when she collected the dog next morning. How old was the daughter? Charley's age? A playmate for him? Fern's head swam with thoughts of how embarrassing it could be.

The first time Fern had seen them together was in a wine bar in Guildford. She had dashed in for change for the parking meter and there they were, tucked away in a romantic corner, she golden, glowing and drooling, he dark and distinguished. Rachel hadn't seen her and at the time Fern had thought little of it, only mildly relieved that she wasn't pursuing her brother any more and had found someone else. So it could have been an entirely innocent liaison, except that 'entirely innocent' couldn't be applied to the next time she had spotted them, parked bumper to bumper in a rural lay-by, both in one car, locked in a passionate embrace. Lovers didn't tryst in lay-bys unless they had something to hide, and now she knew they had. Rachel's lover was married!

'And it's none of my business,' Fern murmured under her breath as she tore at a cardboard box, though she wondered why she should feel so disorientated about her discovery tonight. She didn't like Rachel very much anyway, and he wasn't a consideration, but it was the situation, maybe. Her wonderful marriage to Ralph had been snatched away from her so cruelly, leaving her raw and sensitive to anyone who abused the sanctity of marriage. Some people didn't know how lucky they were.

'Uncle Tim wouldn't have done that,' Charley said the next morning at breakfast.

Fern had toned down the story for the sake of her young son, and simply told him that the farmer had found Sacha lost and put her up for the night and that his kind daughter had fed her and would look after her till they collected her this morning.

'Uncle Tim would have brought her home,' he went on between mouthfuls of cereal.

Yes, Uncle Tim was quite a hero, and sadly it was one of the reasons Fern had left him. She and Charley had lived with her older brother since Ralph's tragic death three years ago. He'd been her strength and solace over the years, but she had seen Charley grow closer and closer to her brother. It was more of a father-son relationship than uncle and nephew, and Fern could see trouble ahead. Though Tim claimed he was a dedicated bachelor, he might succumb to love one day and want to marry and have a family of his own, and then Charley would have to take a back seat in his uncle's affections; and the boy had had enough heartache in his life already.

'Yes, but Uncle Tim knows where we live,' Fern reasoned, 'and that farmer didn't know where Sacha came from.'

'Is he a nice farmer?'

Fern wouldn't have burst his bubble for the world. 'He must be to put her to bed in his nice warm barn.' Instead of shooting her, Fern wryly thought. That was something, she supposed. Funny, but when she had seen him in the wine bar he'd looked a world away from being a farmer. He had appeared more like a successful stockbroker—superbly tailored, his dark hair expertly groomed, an air of success about him. Even last night in the gloom and after suffering a fall from his horse he'd looked elegant and affluent. Certainly not a gentleman farmer, though.

'How old is his daughter?'

'That didn't come into the conversation,' Fern told him with a laugh, 'but maybe about ten going on thirty-five by the looks of him. Hurry up with your breakfast, Charley; we don't want to be late. Sacha must be missing you by now.'

While Charley hunted around for his boots Fern cleared the breakfast things and reflected that the dog had been a wise gift from Tim to help Charley settle into his new home. His first thought had been a puppy, but after visiting the dog refuge he had taken pity on forlorn Sacha, who, though fully grown, was still young and spirited and desperately in need of love.

Aren't we all? Fern breathed to herself as she flicked her fingers through her mass of long, curly brown hair in front of the hall mirror. She didn't look as she ought to after the tragic loss in her life. She looked as young and attractive as she had when she had first married Ralph; it was an effect she had struggled to hang on to for self-preservation. But inside she felt as a widow ought to look—drawn and pale and pinched. Her son was her life and she was happy with that, but there were times— lonely times when Charley was safely tucked up in bed— when she wondered if that was how it was going to be forever.

Guiltily she thrust the thought away from her and called out to Charley to hurry up.

They drove up to Bourne Hall, rather than cutting across the meadow. Fern didn't want any more trouble.

Bourne Hall was an ivy-clad Georgian mansion, and the surrounding grounds so beautifully dressed even in the ravages of a frosty January that Fern wondered if it was a working farm, but, not knowing much of country matters, only gave it a passing thought. She was more occupied with the sudden realisation of why Rachel had been so enthusiastic about her buying the cottage. They weren't close friends, but knew each other because of Tim's partnership in the engineering company. Rachel did a bit of secretarial work sometimes for her father— only sometimes, because work interfered with her social calender. When she had heard that Fern was interested in buying Meadow View she had surprised everyone with an offer to help Fern move in. Now Fern knew why. The Hall overlooked the shallow valley where the cottage nestled, and Rachel's lover's land butted Fern's garden.

Fern was beginning to think her independence wasn't such a good idea after all.

They pulled up on the combed gravel in front of a line of garages that had been converted from a long barn, and Charley was out of the car in a flash and calling for Sacha before Fern could stop him.

Fern got out a trifle less enthusiastically. It was the sort of well-heeled place where children's voices didn't appear welcome, which Fern thought was daft reasoning on her part, because there was a child here, maybe several, and maybe they were kept in the attic under lock and key!

'Hello, you must be Kay.'

Fern swung round and parted her lips in pleasant surprise. The young woman who'd appeared from the side of the long barn was not at all as she had pictured his wife to be. She looked nice. She was young, a strawberry blonde and fresh-faced pretty, and her clothes were almost identical to Fern's—hip-hugging blue denims, baggy sweater and green oiled jacket.

'Yes, I mean no...' She laughed. 'Your husband was——'

'Oh, I'm not James's wife, heaven forbid!' She held out her hand with a grin. 'Sara. I'm Victoria's nanny... Mr Causton's daughter, Victoria.'

'Oh, I'm sorry,' Fern cried, feeling a bit of a fool and taking her hand. 'I'm pleased to meet you, Sara. I was about to say that my name is Fern, not Kay. Ja... Mr Causton had just come off his horse when we met and was confused, I suppose—probably concussed,' she joked, 'and got my name mixed.'

Sara laughed. 'In that case he must be permanently concussed. He called me Sheila for three months before

I finally convinced him I was Sara. He runs his business empire in town blindfolded, but his personal life down here is a different world. He really unwinds—so far that he nearly springs off the end of reality,' she giggled.

'So he's not a farmer?' Fern asked, surprised and yet not after a second's thought. He really hadn't looked the sort to be mucking out or whatever farmers did.

'Merchant banker,' Sara readily told her. 'Hobby farmer in his spare time, which isn't as much as he'd like. He has a manager to run things. He keeps pedigree sheep, which are quite cute, Highland cattle, which are a scream in these parts—they don't look right at all in Surrey—and some evil-looking Vietnamese pot-bellied pigs, which are surprisingly docile and friendly.' Suddenly she looked around her. 'Your brother has disappeared.'

Fern smiled; she was used to this. 'My son,' Fern corrected her as Sara led her down a slight incline between the long barn and the house. 'I'm sorry; he's run off to look for Sacha. I hope he won't get into trouble. Charley is a bit high-spirited.'

'Don't apologise for high spirits,' Sara protested. 'It's natural in well adjusted children. It took me ages to draw Victoria out of her shell. She——'

'It's all right, Sara, I'll deal with this,' came a voice from behind them.

Sara, with an open smile, winked at Fern and turned back to the house.

'Where's Victoria?' James Causton called after her, his warm breath condensing to vapour in the crisp morning air.

'In the drawing-room, drawing,' came the cheery reply.

For the first time Fern saw the man smile, or maybe it was just a grimace at Sara's little joke; whatever, it transformed him. He hadn't been bad-looking to start with, but with his mouth relaxed his whole facial appearance changed into one of heart-thumping no-nonsense good-looking. Somewhere in the far distance Fern was aware of church bells calling in the flock. She turned away and carried on down the incline, not wanting to acknowledge the chemistry that must have swept Rachel off her feet.

'Make sure she stays there,' he called out. 'I don't want her to see the dog going.'

'What did you mean?' Fern asked as he caught her up and fell into step beside her, both of them hunched against the cold in their oiled jackets.

'Victoria rather took to her last night and I had a job convincing her she couldn't keep her.'

'Oh, I'm sorry.'

'Don't be,' he clipped. 'The last thing I want around here is an undisciplined dog.'

'I'm sorry for Victoria, not you,' Fern grumbled. 'And Sacha isn't undisciplined, probably just confused. New home, new owners. Poor love didn't know what was happening last night.'

He said nothing, and Fern vowed inwardly to keep a closer eye on the dog. She didn't want to go through all this again.

'What the devil is going on?' Suddenly James Causton broke into a run, and Fern, hearing the commotion herself, chased after him to a small barn next to the stable block.

The sound of children's voices screaming abuse at each other was overpowered by Sacha's high-pitched hysterical yap. James Causton pulled up in the open doorway and Fern nearly careered into the back of him, skidding on a patch of ice and grabbing at his sleeve to steady herself.

'Charley!' she cried as her wide brown eyes took in the scene. Sacha was three bales of hay above two brawling children, one of them her son. The dog was crouched down, her front paws stretched out in front of her, her golden bottom in the air, yapping as if there were no tomorrow.

'Oh, Charley!' Fern cried again, so embarrassed that she wanted to die. She rushed forward to grab Charley's collar, but James Causton beat her to it. He clasped the boy so tightly that he nearly swung him off his feet, and with his other hand he grabbed at a flurry of squirming pink denim and a mass of straw-tangled blonde hair. Both children were hot, flushed and filthy dirty, and still screeching at each other.

'Sacha's mine...'

'She's Penny now... Daddy said I could keep her!'

'Who the devil is this?' James Causton's voice bellowed round the barn.

'My son,' Fern told him quickly, rushing to rescue Charley from his clutches. She pulled him into her arms, but he pulled away, ready to lurch again at Victoria if need be.

'Mummy, Mummy! She said she's keeping Sacha!'

'It's all right, darling, Sacha is yours——'

'Mummy, Mummy,' the little girl mimicked so derisively that a silence swooped down on all of them; even Sacha collapsed on to her belly, muted. The child had her audience and she drew a deep breath before shouting hurtfully, 'You... sniffy... little... wimp——'

'That's enough, Victoria!' James Causton thundered.

Fern stared in alarm at the child, who certainly wasn't more than Charley's age but had the maturity of...of a thirty-five-year-old. Shocked, she drew Charley protectively towards her again; this time the boy buried his face in her jacket and started to sob uncontrollably.

Sacha whimpered and scrambled down from the bales and flattened herself at Fern's feet. Fern bit her lip and stared at James Causton and was so perturbed at the sight of his uncertainty that her eyes filled with tears.

'Vicky...' A soft voice came from the doorway. They all turned, and Sara stepped into the stuffy barn. She crouched down beside the little girl and took her hand, and the calming influence on the child was instant. 'Annie has just taken some cookies from the oven, so why don't you and Charley come——'

'And Penny...'

'Sacha!' Charley croaked through a sob, his last act of defiance torn from his quivering mouth.

'Sacha,' Sara repeated firmly, and Victoria pouted rebelliously. 'Her name is Sacha and she belongs to Charley, and if you really love her and want to see her again you must stop calling her Penny. Charley won't bring her again if you don't, and you want to see her again, don't you?'

The child nodded meekly.

'Come on, then, both of you.' She stood up and held her other hand out for Charley, who hesitated, clutching tighter at Fern and looking up at her for guidance.

'Cookies sound good to me.' She smiled down at him.

Charley relaxed and went to Sara, who clasped his hand and gave him such a sunny smile of encouragement that it would have melted an iceberg. 'Can Sacha come too?' he asked plaintively.

James Causton let out a sigh of resignation at the flushed, expectant faces turned in his direction, and before he had time to give his consent Sacha beat him to it. With a yelp of excitement she was on her feet and across the barn in a flash. Sara led them all away like the Pied Piper of Hamelin.

'Some Nobel Peace Prize winner you have there,' Fern complimented.

James Causton raked his hand through his dark hair. 'You can say that again. She's worth her weight in gilt-edged.'

They looked at each other across the straw-strewn barn.

'I'm sorry.' They both spoke at once, but whereas Fern laughed immediately afterwards James Causton's face stayed as immobile as a mountain. She realised he was quite shaken by the whole experience, but Fern wasn't giving him any sympathy votes. She couldn't forget Rachel and that passionate embrace.

'I didn't realise the dog belonged to your son,' he said solemnly.

'Would it have made any difference?' she asked flintily. From the corner of her eye she saw a length of rope lying in the straw. Sacha would have hated being tied up all night. It strengthened her resolve not to give this man an inch.

'Yes, it would. I wouldn't have deprived a child of his pet. I wish you had told me last night.'

'You didn't give me a chance.'

A half-smile passed across his well defined lips. 'I was a bit rattled, wasn't I?'

' "Rattled" is an understatement.'

'I'm not used to being thrown off my horse. My pride was a bit shaken.'

'Yes, and I suppose your pride is pretty important to you.'

His dark eyes locked into hers at the gibe, and it made Fern feel surprisingly unsettled. She broke the contact and bent down to pick up the length of rope, her long, curly hair tumbling around her face as she did it. She brushed it impatiently aside as she straightened up.

'Did you tie her up with this?'

He stepped forward and took the rope from her hand, and their fingers brushed, and though the contact was only slight Fern felt it through the length of her body. Her first thought was a gnawing sympathy for Rachel, of all people. To be romantically involved with this man must be something hard to handle.

'I had to,' he started to explain as he wound the rope into a hank. 'It's a long piece, as you can see. She had plenty of room to roam. I couldn't risk her getting out. The barn isn't totally secure and I have sheep close to lambing.' He nodded across the yard. 'They're just over there.' His explanation was so softly timbred and persuasive that as he spoke Fern felt that unease again.

She shifted her feet. 'I'd better get back,' she said softly.

'Yes, your husband must be wondering what's keeping you.'

'I . . . I don't . . .' Suddenly she felt stifling hot in the confines of the sweet-smelling barn. 'I . . . haven't . . .' Her voice gave out and a grim silence closed around them till he broke it.

'You're not married?' he suggested quietly, and surely not with interest?

Fern's eyes blinked rapidly at her soaring imagination, but she was dealing with an adulterer here, so was it any wonder that she was on alert?

'My...my husband died three years ago,' she told him flatly.

There were no words of sympathy like everyone else always offered when told, just a brow raised in surprise and a quizzical murmur. 'A widow?'

Fern repelled a shudder, as she frequently did when faced with her status. 'I hate that word,' she told him, lifting her chin, and meeting his gaze and holding it.

'I don't think there is another word for it.'

'No...there isn't,' Fern admitted with a small sigh, and then forced an equally small smile. 'But I wish there were, one that didn't make me sound so ancient.'

He smiled faintly with her and then abruptly turned and threw the rope on to a bale of hay.

'Then my apologies for last night are twofold.'

Fern clenched her fists. 'I don't need your sympathy,' she iced back, her full lips retracting the smile.

He looked at her again, his dark eyes narrowing. 'I didn't offer it,' he drawled. 'I was simply emphasising my apology. It's not easy bringing a child up on your own and I must have caused you some stress last night.'

If that wasn't sympathy Fern didn't know what was, but she didn't argue. 'It isn't easy,' she said. 'Some people don't realise just how lucky they are.'

That was a dig in the right direction, she thought as she said it, but wasted on him because he didn't know to what she was referring. But if he had a conscience, which she doubted he had, it might have stirred something inside him.

'Yes, quite,' he clipped drily, and Fern wondered. 'So
as you haven't a husband to rush back to let me offer
you a coffee and one of Annie's cookies, consolation
for my cavalier attitude last night.' He didn't wait for
an answer but simply strode out of the barn, expecting
her to follow, which she did. She didn't want to meet
Annie, knowing what she did, but better to get it over
with now and pray that an invitation for a coffee morning
or whatever didn't follow. She wanted no involvement
with the Causton family.

Funny, but she couldn't imagine his wife being called
Annie, she mused as they went back up to the house.
More like a Lucrezia—Borgia!—if his and his daugh-
ter's conduct was anything to go by!

The warm country kitchen was a pleasant surprise to
Fern. It was huge, as was the whole house, but cosily
furnished in a way she planned for her own kitchen.
There was lots of limed oak and shining copper and an
oak settle by the recessed double Aga. The floor was of
polished quarry tiles, and, while Fern had thrown down
a worn Axminster in front of her Aga, this kitchen floor
was scattered with expensive Turkish rugs. Sacha was
coiled on the one nearest the warmth. Charley and
Victoria, looking scrubbed and positively angelic, were
sprawled at a massive refectory table in the centre of the
room, stuffing biscuits and drawing furiously on wodges
of paper with a hundred different felt-tip pens. Sara was
leaning on the fridge in the corner, chatting happily on
the phone, and gave them a wave as they entered the
room from the barn door off the courtyard.

'Coffee and biscuits in the snug, Annie,' James
Causton ordered the homely middle-aged lady who was
drawing out of the oven a fresh batch of cinnamon-

brown biscuits. The delicious smell filled the kitchen, adding to the ambience.

The scenario tugged at Fern's heart-strings. Annie obviously wasn't his wife, but the cook, and probably the housekeeper too, and the whole place smacked of well ordered affluence, achieving an enviable family unit in spite of the arrogance of its master. And where was the mistress? Probably elegantly relaxing in the drawing-room, devouring the Sunday magazines at her leisure. Fern thought of the state she'd left the cottage in—boxes and cartons and heaps of old newspapers screwed up in the corner, stacks of books and ornaments to find homes for...

Fern slid out of her jacket and James Causton took it from her and hung it on the back of the door with his own.

'Daddy, Charley said I can have one of Sacha's puppies when they're born...'

Causton looked in horror at Fern, who gabbled hastily, 'She's not expecting any pups—I hope,' she added tentatively, wondering if that sharp little Victoria knew something she and the dogs' home didn't.

'But she will,' Charley insisted, glancing anxiously at his mother. 'Victoria said that Sacha is a girl and soon she'll find a boy and they'll do something and have babies.'

Fern nearly fainted. She wasn't ready for this yet. Charley was only six!

'Sara, get off that infernal phone, will you?' James deflected, 'And do what you are paid to do—look after children.' He strode from the room, with Fern following and glancing nervously back at Sara, who was grinning and casually saying goodbye to whoever was on the phone. Fern got the distinct impression that James Causton, in spite of his brusque manner, ruled his household with a rod of marshmallow.

Fern's booted feet sank into inches of Aubusson carpet in the cosy room beyond the kitchen, and she apologised quickly.

'I should have taken my boots off.'

'It doesn't matter; I don't.' He nodded to her to take a seat, and Fern sank into a chair by a blazing log fire. 'The children seemed to have settled down. Again I apologise for Victoria's bad behaviour. She can be a precocious little brat at times.'

Fern smiled her surprise. 'That's quite an admission. Most parents don't recognise the brat element in their own children.' If he thought he was going to get polite insistence from her that his daughter wasn't precocious, he was mistaken.

'You have some problems with your own child too,' he suggested, taking a seat on the other side of the fireplace from her.

'I beg your pardon?'

He made church steeples of his fingers and studied her intently, as if she were up in front of a magistrate. 'Your indignation surprises me. You seem to have a very mature outlook on parenthood so long as it isn't your own under scrutiny. Have I touched a sore point?'

'Yes, you have,' Fern told him firmly, refusing to let her anger get the better of her. 'On behalf of my son, I refuse to take responsibility for what happened in the barn. I hate to have to say this, but you are the one with a problem child.'

'I wasn't accusing your son, and on behalf of Victoria I take the blame.' His dark eyes warmed slightly. 'My daughter is mature beyond her years, whereas your son seems immature beneath his years. He appears a bit clingy. How old is he? Six? Seven?'

The temptation to get up and walk out was overruled by one of temptation to stay and put this man down.

'I've never considered him clingy, but, under threat of having his dog taken from him, is it any wonder? Anyway, it's well known that girls are more advanced than boys in childhood, and in most cases that theory runs through adulthood too,' she told him cryptically.

He smiled and was still smiling when Annie came in with a tray of coffee and biscuits. He watched her all the time Annie was pouring the coffee, so intently that it made Fern feel uncomfortable and hot inside.

'How many for lunch, Mr Causton?' Annie asked.

'The usual, Annie,' he murmured abstractedly, still watching her.

Fern looked away, out of the French windows to a frosty patio beyond. Two thoughts whirled in her mind. The first was one so irrational that she could barely accept she had felt it—disappointment that he hadn't suggested she and Charley stay. The second was far more reasonable and down-to-earth—shouldn't Annie have asked the mistress of the house how many people were expected to lunch?

Her imagination was off again. Perhaps he kept his wife in the attic under lock and key, a poor demented soul driven out of her mind by her husband's infidelities.

'Is your wife away?' she asked when Annie had left the room.

He didn't answer straight away, but leaned forward to offer her a biscuit. For a banker his physique was pretty impressive under his checked shirt. His legs were long in dark green cords, the thighs and calves those of a horseman, not one who sat at a desk all day. She acknowledged to herself that he was a very attractive man; interesting, too—a bit of a Jekyll and Hyde. Banker and farmer—a funny sort of combination. She'd bet that Rachel had fallen for the banker side of him.

She took a biscuit and reached for a plate from the tray and then leaned back in her seat. He still hadn't answered, but was smiling, and Fern's undisciplined imagination soared back to the sweet-smelling barn where James Causton was watching her with eyes hooded with desire . . .

Fern crunched furiously into her biscuit and he laughed.

'You've gone very red,' he said quietly behind his coffee-cup.

Fern swallowed the piece of biscuit whole. 'It's the fire,' she croaked and then added quickly, 'Your wife—is she away?'

He took forever to answer and Fern got the impression that he was keeping her waiting to add impact to what he was going to say, but when he finally said it Fern wasn't too surprised. It explained a lot somehow, but what it didn't explain was the sudden pumping of her own heart at those four simple words.

'There is no wife.'

CHAPTER TWO

'OH,' FERN murmured, balancing her plate on her knees and reaching for her coffee-cup from the tray. 'I suppose that explains a lot.'

'Such as?'

Such as why you are having an affair with my brother's partner's daughter, she wanted to blurt, but didn't of course. He only slightly went up in her estimation for not being married. At least he was free to pursue Rachel, but now she knew him better she wondered why he bothered with a little social butterfly like that. Beautiful Rachel might be, but she was short of other worldly attributes—like a brain, for instance. Oh, dear, that was a catty thought. Fern dismissed it instantly. No, she wouldn't give James Causton, banker with a brain, a bigger slice of her estimation—not yet.

'Victoria and her astonishing maturity,' Fern suggested, thinking that if the child had been disciplined by her mother she wouldn't be the way she was.

'Yes, she is sophisticated beyond her years, but in some ways incredibly childish, which must sound like a contradiction, but as a mother yourself I'm sure you know what I mean.'

She nodded her understanding. 'Are you a widower?'

His face crumpled into a grimace. 'Terrible word; it would make me feel ancient too if it were so.'

Fern smiled. 'Well, there isn't another word for it, I'm afraid.'

27

He grinned, and the barn was back in her imagination again, and James Causton was stepping towards her...

'I know, and I'm not one, so labels aren't a problem.'

'But you must have one—a label, I mean. Are you divorced?'

'Not that either.'

'Oh,' Fern murmured again, lowering her eyes to the milky coffee, which had already formed a skin.

'You emit an awful lot of "oh"s,' he commented.

Fern shrugged her narrow shoulders. 'I don't wish to probe.'

'Point taken,' he said dismissively, and offered her another biscuit.

Fern took one, because they were quite delicious. She juggled the plate on her lap and the coffee-cup in her hands to accept the biscuit. So he hadn't a wife, but he wasn't a widower and wasn't divorced, so that only left separated. An excuse for an affair, but only just.

'When did you move into Meadow View?' he asked, leaning back and studying her once again.

Fern had the feeling that by the time she left here he would know her life story inside-out and backwards and she would know precious little of his.

'Yesterday. Last night was our first night in the old cottage.'

'Now you've made me feel doubly bad for my behaviour last night.'

'You have nothing to feel bad about,' she offered without malice. 'You weren't to know, and Sacha's behaviour must have really annoyed you.'

'But I didn't even give you a chance to explain,' he insisted.

'The circumstances didn't really warrant it. You were more concerned with your pride.' Her eyes twinkled and he smiled.

'Hmm, an instance of pride coming *after* the fall.'

'Did you hurt yourself?'

'No, only the pride hurt. I thought I knew my horse better.'

'I did rather startle him with that whistle of mine.'

'Yes, some whistle from such a little thing.'

His eyes flicked over her body and Fern squirmed inside, wishing in that instant that she weren't shabbily dressed in jeans and home-knit sweater and wondering why he made her feel that way—self-conscious. She finished her biscuit, and suddenly the room was so quiet that she felt even more ill at ease. With the coffee-spoon she skimmed the skin from her coffee and drank it quickly.

'I'd better go,' she said as she put her cup and saucer back on the tray. It was remarkable, but she didn't want to go. She could sit here all day in the warmth and comfort of his sumptuous home. She remembered Rachel, and it burst the bubble of warmth. 'I'm expecting a friend,' she added.

To her surprise his eyes darkened, and Fern couldn't think why, and was even more surprised when he said, 'A man friend?'

'A friend,' she repeated, intentionally skirting that one for no other reason than the fact that the so-called friend was one he was very intimate with—Rachel. Fern hadn't been able to put her off, and she was coming around to give her a hand to unpack. The thought depressed her, because now Fern realised why the offer had been made—not to help her out, but simply to get closer to her lover. She had probably arranged to drop in on him while she was in the area anyway. Quite something, that, Fern mused as they went back to the kitchen. Inside she felt the stirrings of something she had never suspected she was capable of feeling—envy. James Causton, in spite of a bucketful of flaws in his character, was a very attractive man.

'Ohh, do we have to go?' Charley whined. 'It's nice here. I want to stay. I don't *want* to go back to that awful place!'

Fern vowed she'd put him on bread and water for a month for that. She nearly blurted out that they had to go because Rachel was coming round, but she dared not mention that name in front of Causton, and besides, her son wasn't too keen on Rachel either and that wouldn't bribe him away.

Again the indefatigable Sara came to the rescue, with back-up in the form of Annie with a bag of cookies for Charley to take home. As she helped the boy on with his coat she said, 'You can come again, Charley, any time you like, and Vicky and I would love to come and see you and Sacha in your new home, so perhaps we can call in soon.'

'We'll see him tomorrow,' Victoria blurted out. 'Charley goes to my school, Daddy.'

James Causton looked at his daughter in disbelief, and Fern bridled. It was an expensive private school, but not *exclusive*. Fern could only afford it because of the hefty compensation awarded to her son for the loss of his father. Ironically, Ralph could never have afforded to send his son to such a school, even though he'd had what the court called 'great expectations' before his death.

'Thank you for the coffee, Annie,' Fern got in quickly before Causton could make a comment. 'And you're welcome any time, Sara. Goodbye, Vicky.'

'Victoria,' the child corrected primly.

Under cover of slipping into her coat, Fern pulled a face at Charley, who giggled behind his felt-tip-stained fingers.

'Thank you for looking after Sacha last night, Mr Causton.'

'James,' he insisted. 'It was no trouble, Kay.'

'Fern,' she corrected, and, taking her son's hand, she said as she opened the back door, 'Come on, Fred, let's go!'

She heard Sara explode into giggles—and was that James Causton actually laughing too?

Fern was losing her patience with Rachel. It was so obvious why she was here, and it wasn't to help with the unpacking.

'Didn't know you were so fascinated by wildlife,' Fern couldn't help caustically remarking. Rachel hadn't shifted two paces from the back-bedroom window which directly overlooked the Causton fields and which in fact gave a fair view of the Hall as well. It was still too far away to detect signs of life, but Fern supposed when you were in love the sight of your lover's roof was enough to get you through another day.

'Oh, I think this place is lovely,' Rachel cooed. 'You're so lucky, Fern, you really are.'

Stifling a crippling retort to that, Fern shifted a box of linen towards her. 'Can you stack this linen in the airing cupboard *if* you can drag your attention away from *Lolium perenne* for five minutes.'

Rachel whirled round from the window as if she'd been caught in the act. 'What's that?'

'Grass!' Fern retorted as she slammed out of the room.

'Uncle Tim's here!' Charley shouted as she stepped into the kitchen. He pelted for the back porch, and Fern supposed this was the sort of place where no one came to the front door.

Resigned to not getting any sorting-out done today, she filled the kettle and put it on the hob.

'Rachel pulling her weight, is she?' Tim asked after swinging Charley around the kitchen and finally dropping him down into a chair as if he were a sack of coal.

Fern gave her brother a rueful look. 'What do you think?'

Tim grinned and set about tickling Sacha's tummy as she sprawled contentedly in front of the Aga.

'It was nice of her to offer to come, anyway.'

Out of sight of Tim, Fern raised her eyes skywards. Little did he know the real reason why the offer had been made—a certain James Causton in close proximity.

'She's joining the company full-time at the end of the month,' Tim told her as he stood up and came to stand next to her as she made the tea. 'Robert thinks it's about time she had a proper job and earned her keep.'

'Not before time,' Fern remarked. 'Her father has spoilt her all these years. How do you feel about her working for the company?'

Tim shrugged his broad shoulders. 'I'm not bothered so long as she knuckles down. So how's it going here?'

Fern was glad of the change of subject. It was turning out to be the longest Sunday in history. After her visit to the Causton mansion this morning she had really thrown herself into getting the cottage organised and homely. Fortunately the new fitted carpets had been laid during the week and the curtains she'd made herself weeks ago had been hung and the removal men had kindly put the furniture where she wanted it, but there were still mountains of miscellaneous stuff to be put away. Then lunch, though Charley had eaten so many of Annie's cookies that he'd hardly touched a thing, so lunch had been a waste of time. And then Rachel had arrived, hair swept up into a cascade on the top of her head, which had looked encouraging but the rest of her hadn't. A peach silk shirt and colour co-ordinated cashmere cardigan to perfectly complement her red-gold hair, and stream-lined off-white leggings to *perfectly* complement the silk shirt, was *hardly* the outfit for un-packing dusty old boxes!

Fern wondered when she was ever going to get down to some serious work. She had a business to run and had orders to get out.

'Come and see my bedroom, Uncle Tim,' Charley cried and whisked Tim away up the stairs that led off the kitchen.

'I've just made tea!' Fern wailed plaintively as they disappeared. Sacha eyed her dolefully and then stood up, shook herself, and ambled up the stairs after the others. '*Et tu, Brute*,' Fern mumbled and poured herself a tea and slumped down by the Aga. What a day!

Tim and Rachel left soon after, and as Fern and Charley went round the cottage, drawing the curtains to keep in the warmth as night fell, Fern reflected how amazing children were. Charley hadn't said a word to Tim or Rachel about spending the morning up at the hall. The next morning she thought she understood why.

* * *

'Charley, will you please hurry up?' Fern yelled up the stairs. 'We're going to be late! Oh, 'struth!' she moaned as the phone rang.

'James Causton,' the voice announced. Fern's first reaction was to look around for Sacha, who was happily gnawing a Bonio on the rug in front of her mother substitute, the Aga. 'Bad news, I'm afraid,' he went on, and Fern's heart thudded. 'As you were here yesterday I thought you ought to know that Victoria is down with chicken-pox.'

Fern fell on the chair by the phone. 'That explains it,' she said wearily. 'Charley's been grizzling since I woke him this morning. He says he's got a sore throat. I just thought he was making it up—new school and all that.'

'Victoria's rash broke out in the night. She had the sore throat a few days ago. Sara says half the children at school are down with it. It looks like quite an epidemic.'

At that moment Charley staggered down the stairs, looking pale and wan, his school tie all askew, his brown blazer half off his shoulders. Fern's eyes filled with tears.

'Just a minute,' she breathed down the phone, and covered the mouthpiece. 'Charley, go back to bed, poppet. I'll be up in a minute.'

The little boy didn't argue but turned and desolately climbed back up the stairs.

'I'm sorry, I'll have to go,' Fern told James. 'Thanks for letting me know.'

'Fern!'

'Yes?'

'Look, I'm not going up to town for a few days. Victoria is quite a handful when she's ill and…well…she needs me, so I'm here. I mean, if you need anything don't hesitate to call.' He gave her his number and Fern jotted it down, her hand shaking as she did it.

To her dismay the tears were rolling down her cheeks now, and she was glad James wasn't here to witness it. This was Charley's first real illness, and it brought it home to her that she was going to have to cope with it on her own.

'Fern?'

She gulped. 'Yes, I've got it, and thank you for letting me know, and thank you for being so...so neighbourly.'

'It was the least I could do. Goodbye.'

Fern sat cradling the receiver in her hands before putting it back. Ungratefully, she wished he hadn't bothered to call, because somehow it emphasised her loneliness and it also strengthened the feeling she had that he felt sorry for her. How easy to offer his services when he had such a good back-up at home.

As Fern hurried upstairs to her sick son she reasoned that she felt the resentment because of what she knew about him and Rachel, and that wasn't particularly fair, but nevertheless she couldn't help feeling that way.

Charley sailed through his illness, much to Fern's surprise and delight. The first day had been the worst, with the child alternating between sleep and restlessness, and he'd had Fern dashing up and down the stairs every five minutes. By the time the spots had appeared two weeks later Charley was raring to go back to school, but the school definitely didn't want him back yet.

'How's the patient?'

Fern was standing back against a mossy bank when she heard the horse and rider approaching behind her in the narrow lane. Fern immediately slipped the lead on Sacha and heeled her and waited for him to pass, but he didn't.

'Fine, how's yours?'

'Fretful,' James told her, sliding out of the saddle to join her.

Sacha shot to her feet and wagged her tail furiously. James patted her head. 'You remember.'

Fern wished she didn't *remember*. She'd like to forget he was Rachel's lover.

'Are the spots still driving her wild?' As she made her enquiry, Fern wondered at it. There he was, every inch the handsome banker and landowner, in his expertly tailored riding gear—black jodhpurs, and a black cashmere roll-necked sweater under a stylishly cut oiled jacket that hadn't been purchased at a surplus store, where Fern's jacket had come from—and she was enquiring after his daughter's spots!

'No, she's just bored rigid. Needs the company of other children. She should be back at school by now but she picked up a bug from somewhere on top of the chicken-pox.'

Fern secretly prayed he wouldn't ask her to bring Charley up for an hour. She couldn't bear that.

'Look, I've got to go.' Sacha was restless now and straining on the lead, and Fern had only just popped out for five minutes. 'I shouldn't have left Charley, but I had to dash out with Sacha. She needs exercising.'

'I'll walk back with you.'

There was just room for them to walk side by side up the lane, with the horse trailing behind. Fern let Sacha off the lead and she romped up the lane ahead of them. Fern walked briskly because she was tense at having left Charley.

'Are you all right?' James asked as they reached the gate of the cottage.

Charley called out from the front door and waved. Fern visibly relaxed, and James noticed.

'I wish you had phoned for help,' James said with a frown. 'You're totally isolated here——'

'I've managed,' she said curtly and then smiled an apology at her abruptness. 'I'm sorry for snapping. It's just that I hate leaving Charley, even for a few minutes, but Sacha won't...won't do it in the garden.'

James laughed, and on a crazy impulse Fern asked him in for a coffee.

She went into the cottage while he tethered his horse to a post just inside the garden, and wondered at her nerve at asking him in. It had been a silly thing to do. If Rachel dropped in...but no, she wouldn't. And it wasn't because of that, more for the interpretation James Causton might put on the invitation.

'How many spots has Victoria got?' Charley asked with morbid relish.

'I haven't counted them,' James told him, slipping out of his coat. 'But I will when I get back. How many have you got?'

'We counted them last night and I've got a hundred and one and lots more because my hair is so thick that Mummy couldn't find them all.'

James winced and smiled at Fern, who turned away to hang up their coats in the tiny hall. Well, that would put paid to any romantic notion James might see in the offer of a cup of coffee—that was if he'd had one in the first place.

'Come through to the kitchen,' she said, and then to her son, 'Keep Sacha out of my studio, Charley.'

The boy caught the dog in the sitting-room and dragged her by the scruff of her neck to the kitchen.

'You're an artist?' James asked with interest.

'No. I wish I had the time for such a luxury.' Fern grinned ruefully. 'Do you want to see what I'm trying to earn a living at?' As soon as she said it she wished she hadn't. She reminded herself that he was just her neighbour, but he was a male neighbour and Rachel's lover and . . . and actually, when she came to think of it, she hadn't anything to worry about, not from him; she was no competition for Rachel's sophisticated looks.

'I'd be very interested.'

'Children's clothes,' she told him proudly, waving her hand in the direction of her cutting table, which almost filled the room. It was covered in paper patterns and stacks of brightly coloured cotton fabrics. The walls were lined with boards and, pinned to them, the designs she was working on. Leaning against the walls were rolls of fabric—dyed cottons and denims, velvets, and some of the luxury satins she was experimenting with.

'Mail order,' she told him. 'I cut the fabric and send it out in kit form. All the purchaser has to do is sew up the seams. These are my first orders. I started advertising before I moved in and sent out catalogues, and all these orders were here when I arrived. I design all my own stuff. No zips, no complicated button-throughs. Simple, snazzy, over-the-head wear for trendy kids and frazzled mothers. Cheap, too—cuts out the middleman.' She picked up a swath of scarlet satin. 'If it all goes well I'm thinking of trying party wear, not in kit form, but making the orders up myself.'

'Very time-consuming,' he told her as he walked around the table, picking up pieces of fabric and examining them. 'You'd be better off putting the work out and concentrating on your designs.' He looked up at her suddenly. 'Delegate.'

Fern steeled herself. She hadn't exactly expected him to rave about her infant cottage industry, but she hadn't expected he'd start trying to run it for her in five seconds flat either.

'Where do you advertise?'

'The local Press.'

He looked positively derisive at that, which annoyed Fern intensely. 'Go nationwide and in a couple of months go international. If you're going to do something, do it big.'

'I'm not the only one doing this sort of thing, you know!' she retorted.

'Competition is always a good thing, keeps you on your toes. Speculate to accumulate.'

Fern went round the table and snatched the sample he was holding from his hand. She was burning inside. 'And sometimes to speculate is to dissipate.'

'Defeatist,' he cut back shrewdly.

'I know my limitations.'

'Don't even think about limitations.'

'Well, I happen to be living them,' she told him drily.

'Charley?'

'Yes, Charley. If you hadn't noticed, I'm operating a single-parent family unit here. I'm doing this because I have no choice of doing anything else. I need to be with him. I need to be here when he comes home from school. I need to——'

'Live your life for him?'

'Yes, live my life for him!' she blurted hotly.

Suddenly his hand came up and touched her chin, his thumb smoothing away the tension from her jaw. Her whole being nearly melted under the touch. 'And not have a life of your own?' he questioned so smoothly and suggestively that a *frisson* of scary awareness nettled down her spine.

Fern was also suddenly aware of Charley moving around upstairs, out of sight and out of earshot and for a second out of her life. James Causton was so close to her that she felt a crazy stirring deep inside her. She could smell him and feel the warmth of his body, and she hadn't been so exposed to that sort of awareness for such a long time.

'And do you have a life of your own?' he repeated, his voice soft and suggestive and verging on mild mockery.

The room seemed to close in on her and all sorts of wild thoughts erupted inside her. Her needs that she'd bottled deep inside for three years suddenly seemed painfully sensitive and close to the surface of her skin. But she had no right even to think about them.

'My time will come,' she breathed softly.

'Maybe it already has.'

His head moved towards hers, and in that second Fern experienced sheer panic. A lightning thought crossed her mind that if his lips touched hers life would never be the same again.

She jerked her head back and moved away from him, yet not knowing what her intentions were after that.

He gave her a half-smile, a knowing smile, and picked up the sample she had snatched from his hand. He ran his fingers over the appliquéd front of the bright blue playsuit and Fern watched as he did it, her liquid brown eyes concentrating hard on the garment, rather than braving herself to look at him again. She felt sick inside, but couldn't succumb to it, wouldn't allow herself to acknowledge that his presence and his words were disturbing her deeply.

'You have a talent,' he told her quietly. 'You should take advantage of it, all the way, not half-measures.'

Then she did brave herself to look into his eyes, and what she saw made her wonder if he was speaking of her talent as a designer or something else. She didn't like games like this. It made her feel vulnerable and unable to cope. She wasn't sure of anything any more. She'd been too long out of the flirting game.

And he was flirting, she felt sure. At least she was still able to recognise that when confronted with it. But, attractive as he was, and available as he was, she couldn't submit, because she knew the sort of man he was—one who toyed with women's affections. One woman in particular, who was too close to home for Fern's comfort.

'Do you still want a coffee?' she asked, secretly hoping he'd refuse.

He smiled. 'It's what you asked me in for, isn't it?'

'Well, I certainly didn't invite you in to shoot my project down in flames.' She hoped her tone of voice quashed any ideas he had that she'd asked him in for anything else.

He looked amused. 'As a merchant banker it's what I do. Sometimes it runs into my private life too.'

She was nearly flattered to think she was part of his private life, but so was the boy who delivered his papers, she supposed.

'And as a merchant banker I'm sure you have better things to do than advise small fry like me.'

'Don't underestimate your capabilities, Fern,' he said seriously. 'That's the first mistake in business. Don't forget there's many a shrewd banker behind small fry with talent, urging them on to their first million.'

Fern smiled wryly. 'Is that an offer to back me?'

He grinned. 'I only deal in commercial——'

'Big boys and safe bets,' she interrupted. 'As I thought. You haven't the nerve to put your money where your mouth is.'

He looked slightly taken aback by that, and Fern smiled and relaxed. 'I was only teasing. I'll go and make the coffee.'

He followed her into the kitchen. 'If you want a loan I can easily arrange it. I could put you in touch with a sympathetic banker.'

Fern turned from the sink, where she was filling the kettle. She wasn't at all offended by his offer, because his tone hadn't been patronising. He was only trying to help, but she felt she had to put him right.

'Thanks, but no, thanks. You see, I have money enough. This house wasn't cheap and isn't mortgaged and I can afford to send my son to the best school in the area——'

'I wasn't implying——'

'I know,' she interjected quickly. She smiled, because he was looking so worried that he had upset her. She took a deep breath, because she wanted to explain. 'My husband was an engineer. He worked on the oil rigs. We had a good lifestyle in Aberdeen before the accident—a nice home, everything we could wish for. The accident wasn't his fault. . .' As she spoke she could feel the ache of loss inside her spreading, the tears irritating the back of her eyelids, but she wanted to go on. 'Three other men were killed with him, all family men. The courts were sympathetic and the company admitted negligence. We were all compensated enough to keep ourselves and our children for the rest of our lives...and...so it should be,' she finished in a whisper.

She turned back to the sink and her hands were shaking as she jammed the lid on the kettle.

'But it's never enough, is it?' he said quietly behind her, and she knew he didn't mean money, and she was glad of that.

Fern bit her lip and determinedly she thrust the kettle down on the hob. She was clear-eyed when she looked at him, her chin slightly raised from her cowl-necked sweater.

'No, it's never enough,' she admitted hoarsely. Wiping her hands down her jeans, she smiled again. 'Keep an eye on that for a minute while I check to see if Charley is OK. It's gone awfully quiet up there.'

Her son was curled on the bed with Sacha coiled into his back, and they both slept peacefully. Fern placed a hand gently on her son's forehead. He was such a brave little soldier, one minute roaring to go back to school, the next like this, exhausted. He still wasn't well, but he tried so hard—sometimes, she suspected, for her sake more than his own. She pulled the duvet up over his legs and then quietly crept out of the room.

James was searching cupboards for two cups, and Fern felt an unnecessary pull at her heart as she came back down the stairs into the kitchen. It was strange seeing a man, apart from her brother, who was family anyway, moving about in such a domesticated way in her own home. She could almost laugh out loud at that thought. James Causton was hardly domesticated. But it was still unnerving to see him doing something so commonplace in her kitchen, and it sharpened her loneliness till the ache honed to a physical pain.

'Here,' she said, going to a wall cupboard and taking out two mugs.

'Is he asleep?' He watched as she spooned coffee granules into the mugs.

'Flat out.' She glanced at the clock. 'Not quite four o'clock, which means he'll be up late tonight and I won't get any work done.'

'A woman's work is never done,' he murmured, as if to make conversation, and Fern suddenly realised they were trying to make conversation. Somehow everything had suddenly shifted course, and she didn't understand why. Silently she made the coffee, stirring the hot water briskly as she poured it over the granules.

'Sugar? Milk?'

'Neither.'

She turned to hand him one of the mugs and he was standing by the Aga, the toby jug in his hands—Ralph's toby jug. It was one of the first things she'd unpacked and placed on the shelf over the Aga.

She handed him his coffee and he put the jug back to free his hand to take it.

Fern laughed hesitantly. 'Ralph bought me that when I was expecting Charley. If I had a son I wanted to call him Toby. Ralph said we should wait and see what his ears were like before deciding on giving him a handle like that. I didn't know what he meant, and he bought me that to prove his point.'

James smiled. 'So you called him Charley.'

Fern nodded, her eyes bright with the memories. 'His ears were enormous,' she laughed. 'They aren't so bad now he's got hair.'

'He's a very good-looking boy; you must be very proud of him.'

'I am,' Fern murmured. They drank their coffee, and there was that terrible silence again, and the only thing Fern could put it down to was that in fact they really had nothing in common except their children. She had been mistaken in thinking he had been flirting with her before; maybe she had wished it.

'I'd better go,' he said at last, and Fern was relieved, because all the time he was here she was getting more confused. How could she have possibly wished he had been flirting with her?

'Yes, it will be dark soon, and if I remember rightly you haven't got headlights on your horse.'

It was a very feeble joke, and he obviously thought so too, because he made no comment and his mouth didn't move.

He pulled on his jacket in the hall and Fern opened the door for him. A chill blast hit her, and, coupled with the thought that once she shut this door on him he would be gone, the icy chill seemed to penetrate to her bones. What on earth was happening to her?

'Thanks for the coffee.' He paused in the doorway, hunching against the cold. 'When Charley's better I'll send Sara down to baby-sit and I'll take you out to dinner.'

The offer was almost thrown into the wind, as if he didn't really care if it blew back into his face. Which it did.

Fern steeled every nerve in her body, and this wasn't even to do with Rachel.

'Thanks, but no, thanks,' she said tightly.

He half turned to face her.

'Why?'

The question completely threw her, and for a wild second she nearly threw Rachel back at him, but, as she had so rightly assessed before, this was nothing to do with Rachel. It was to do with everything but— Charley... and the toby jug... her independence... and her little business, which he probably thought was going nowhere.

'Because I don't need your sympathy or your pity——'

To her shock his hand lifted and gripped her chin and his eyes locked into hers. 'I don't give my sympathy and pity to beautiful wealthy widows...' And then his mouth closed over hers and the kiss spun her out into the night, upwards to some unknown starry galaxy that called out for her. His lips were hot and passionate, confident and persuasive, and her lips beneath were suddenly whipped into an ecstasy she hadn't known existed.

Her senses were not her own; they flamed urgently, summoned from deep inside her, where they had lain in a torpor for so long. She didn't want it to end, yet she did, because confusion reigned. She wasn't Fern McKay anymore, widow and mother of a six-year-old, but a stranger to herself.

Slowly he moved his mouth from hers, tantalisingly drawing on her bottom lip as a last withdrawal.

When he spoke his voice was different—lower, softer, huskier. 'And my invitation was only given out for one reason, Fern McKay. I want you out of your cosy domesticity for a few hours because I happen to fancy you like hell!'

Then he was gone, swallowed up into the frosty night air, leaving Fern shivering, and it wasn't with the cold blast of air that whipped her hair around her hot cheeks. That kiss had been something, a combination of everything she lacked in her life: passion, sensuality, warmth. Her heart tightened. But she needed more than that, and the likes of James Causton couldn't give it to her, because kisses like that to him came cheap. He probably dished them out to all and sundry, Rachel Edwards being the current recipient. The thought of the kiss she had witnessed in the lay-by hardened her heart against him, but at least he had been honest, and she couldn't fault him for that. He just fancied her and that was all.

CHAPTER THREE

LIFE was back to normal, if normal existed after that kiss, that invitation, that reason for it.

Fern wasn't even flattered, because now she had the measure of the man. He was a womaniser. Widows, empty-headed social butterflies, James Causton wasn't choosy, but at least he had accepted her refusal. She hadn't seen or heard from him for two weeks, and she had mixed feelings about that. Part of her was relieved that he hadn't pursued it, and a funny little part of her was very slightly disappointed and would have been hugely disappointed if Rachel Edwards hadn't got prior claim to him. Heavens, what an admission, that she was actually attracted to the man. But she wasn't going to step on anyone's toes, least of all Rachel's. All very confusing, Fern often mused as life went on.

The temperature had risen lately, melting away the frost, and then the rain had moved in—days and days of it. Fern was surprisingly affected by it, causing her to feel uncharacteristically down.

So last night she had decided enough was enough. She had no reason to feel low. Charley was well and back to school and thoroughly enjoying it, but what she needed was some time in town. She was running short of velvet cord fabric—there had been a run on it in the cold spell—and why not splurge out on a few luxuries while she was at it? Charley needed some treats after his illness. She'd phoned Tim to ask him to pick Charley up from school and bring him home for his tea, and to feed Sacha and take her out for a run. She'd promised to be back by six at the latest.

Fern frowned as she pulled into the lane that led to Meadow View. There were no lights coming from the cottage, not even a chink through the curtains. She glanced down at the clock on the dashboard. It was half-past five, pouring with rain and pitch-dark. Surely Tim hadn't taken Charley out for his tea? She grinned. She wouldn't put it past him; her brother wasn't very domesticated. She'd kill him if he'd driven Charley into Guildford for a Chinese, though; it always gave him nightmares.

Sacha went wild as Fern let herself into the dark cottage. She switched on the lights, dumped her parcels on the chair, and bent to make a fuss of the dog before she tore at her tights.

'How are you, girl? Did you miss me? Oh, no!'

Fern stared in dismay round the small front hallway. The hall rug was in shreds. Sacha suddenly crouched down with guilt, her tail whacking out a sorry on the carpet. Suddenly Fern realised what had happened.

'You haven't been out, have you?' She opened the front door and Sacha shot out into the darkness. Fern went into the kitchen, slipping off her overcoat and running upstairs with it over her arm. She checked Charley's wardrobe. He always changed out of his uniform as soon as he got in. His blazer wasn't there, and Fern felt an irritating ripple run through her. The idea for Tim to come back here with Charley was to let the dog out and feed her; she'd emphasised that. Fern had given her a good run before going, purposely not leaving till midday so the dog wouldn't be alone for too long.

She ran downstairs and picked up the phone and dialled her brother's number. He must have taken Charley home with him straight from school. Tim barked out the number so severely that Fern held it away from her ear.

'Who's rattled your cage?'

'Sorry, sis.' His voice softened apologetically. 'I'm a bit on edge. I've got Rachel here with me; I'm trying to teach her the rudiments of basic bookkeeping.' His voice went even lower, and Fern could see the tortured smile on his handsome face. 'I'd stand more chance with a chimpanzee.'

Fern grinned. 'You have my sympathy, but what is Charley doing while all this is——?'

'Charley!' Tim spluttered, and then there was a terrible silence, a terrible, ominous silence.

The blood drained from Fern's heart and a murky blackness swirled around her. 'Tim!' Fern croaked, her pulses faint with horror. 'He's there... with you... you did...' Oh, God, no! He hadn't! Fern knew it with a panicky certainty, a mother's intuition, a terrible life-destructive force that paralysed her.

'Fern... dear God... Rachel was here and——'

'You... you forgot!' Fern's insides heaved and the blood of fear rushed to her head. This couldn't be happening! Tim *couldn't* have forgotten!

'It's all right... Fern, don't panic...'

Fern dropped the receiver, a strangled sob scouring her throat, the blood still rushing so fiercely round her head that she rocked dizzily. She shook from head to toe, not knowing what to do or where to turn. Her son, her beloved son, had been out of school...for hours...in the dark...in the rain. The police... She must call the police...

The phone rang. She snatched at it, ready to scream at her brother.

'Fern, you're home, then——'

'Who is this?' she cried.

'James——'

'James!' She couldn't think. This was a nightmare. Not now...not now...she wanted to scream, but she had no voice.

'We have Charley here,' he said calmly.

His cool, almost icy voice sliced through the terror in her head. She was freezing cold now, shivering uncontrollably, her relief washing through her like a waterfall of crushed ice.

'How?' she managed weakly.

'Sara picked up Victoria as usual and found Charley still there.' There was a small pause. 'I'll bring him down later—— '

'No!' Fern blurted hysterically 'I'll come for him now!' She plunged the receiver down and closed her eyes and leaned against the wall to gather her wits together. She had to go now, to prove to herself that he was alive and well, to prove to her son that he was her life. What must have been going through his little mind as he waited and waited? Thank God, oh, thank God for Sara. The relief that swamped her again and again made her feel so sick. She took deep breaths to calm herself, then shakily she went to the kitchen and opened a can of meat for Sacha and called her in. She took more deep breaths as she watched the hungry dog eating. Charley was safe...but he might not have been ... but he was and that was all that mattered in the world.

Picking up her car keys, she went outside, not feeling the rain, not aware that she hadn't an overcoat over the top of her fine wool suit, not feeling anything now but a shocked numbness.

'Is he all right, Annie?' Fern asked anxiously as the smiling housekeeper opened the front door of Bourne Hall to her.

'Why shouldn't he be?'

'I thought ... I thought ...'

Annie laughed as she closed the door behind her. 'And children don't. He's been having a fine old time with Victoria. They've had their tea and they're watching videos upstairs.'

'Can I go up?'

'I'll take you up,' came a voice from across the hall, and James Causton strode towards her. He was dressed in his city clothes, as was Fern, but whereas he looked smooth and elegant Fern felt she looked positively dishevelled after a day in town shopping till she dropped. She wished she hadn't gone now; with all her heart she wished she'd stayed at home where she belonged.

She was silent as she walked beside him up the wide stairway, her eyes straight ahead, refusing to acknowledge the works of art displayed on the walls. She was ridden with guilt for what she had done, and it was obvious that James Causton thought she had cause to be as well. His face was implacable, carved out of stone, his shoulders stiff, his steps precise.

'Hi, Mummy. Victoria has all the Superman movies. She said I can borrow them any time.'

Fern's heart thudded with relief that he wasn't upset in any way. In fact he hadn't even missed her, she realised. He and Victoria were spread-eagled on floor cushions in the pastel-coloured nursery suite, munching apples and fast-forwarding Superman through space.

'This bit's good,' Victoria giggled, slowing the film to where Superman and Lois Lane were in a clinch. The two children rolled in fits of giggles on the floor.

Sara was by the window, curled on a pink velvet *chaise-longue*, the phone pressed to her head.

'I'll have that welded to your ear for your birthday,' James told her, but she didn't hear, just grinned and waved.

Fern felt her tension easing, her shoulders sagging with relief. Charley was warm and safe and happy and in good hands.

'You look as if you could do with a drink.'

Fern turned her pale face to him, surprised by the offer. She realised it was exactly what she needed; her throat felt as if she had been screaming non-stop for hours.

'Thank you, yes, please.'

He shut the door of the nursery suite after him and Fern blurted, 'I'm sorry... I feel so embarrassed...'

'And so you should be,' he said curtly, and without adding any more he led her downstairs.

A log fire blazed in the grate of the Adam-styled fire-place of the sitting-room, another tastefully furnished room of the mansion. The sofas were upholstered in pale cream slubbed silk and the armchairs in a soft green velour; the carpet was pale cream with a muted floral motive at intervals across the wide expanse of room. There were satinwood occasional tables with silver and flowers in bowls displayed on the polished surfaces, and heavy swags of glazed cotton across the windows excluded the dismal dark from the warm, peaceful room. Fern noticed it all in detail, because suddenly she was alive again, because Charley was safe, and could register that this was a home and that what she had at Meadow View wasn't quite that yet.

Fern stood nervously by the fireplace. Upstairs she had felt the tension ease; now it was creeping back again.

'A small gin and tonic,' she replied when he asked what she wanted to drink. She watched him pour it, then a drink for himself. She felt compelled to explain. 'I . . . I went up to London. . . I arranged for Tim to pick Charley up . . .'

'Ah, yes, Uncle Tim.' His voice was so derisive that Fern wasn't sure how to take it.

She swallowed hard. 'Did. . . did Charley say?' She took the drink he handed her and clasped it with two hands.

'Yes, he said.'

Fern nodded. 'I . . . I was distraught when I got back and found he had . . . for-forgotten.'

James Causton eyed her coldly over the rim of his glass. 'Sara said Charley insisted he was coming for him. He didn't.'

He did nothing to hide the disdain in his voice, and Fern sipped her drink nervously, but it did nothing to ease the tension. She knew how it must look—totally irresponsible on her and her brother's part, but so much worse for herself because she was here, embarrassed at having to face this man's scorn.

'I've always been able to trust him before . . .' she murmured painfully, and now she never could again. Her own brother had let her down so badly.

'He said Uncle Tim was coming to pick him up,' James Causton repeated, as if taunting her.

Fern bit her lip, and swallowed some more of her drink.

'He said how he wished he still lived with Uncle Tim.'

Fern shook her head in distress, knowing that if they had still been living with him none of this would have happened. 'I'm beginning to think we should never have left.' She let out a crumpled sigh. 'Tim was so good to us after...after Ralph died. Charley and I moved in with him because...because it seemed the natural thing to do. Everything was as perfect as it could be, but...but it was Charley really. I decided to move out for his sake. They were getting too close. Charley turned to him for everything, which was understandable, but they were more like father and son and I could feel myself losing my grip on my own son.'

She looked up at James, hoping he might understand. Her blood ran cold at the way he was looking at her, coldly, hostilely. Her wide brown eyes flickered down to the glass he held in his hand and she was shocked to see his knuckles, marble-white, gripping the lead crystal. He didn't understand. She was a fool to think he might have done.

'I'm sorry...I'm talking too much...'

'On the contrary. I'm finding it all very enlightening,' he told her icily. 'I don't often make character misjudgements, but there is always a first time.'

Fern flushed deeply and tightened her grip on her glass. The fire was scorching the backs of her legs, but she couldn't move.

'And this Tim, this irresponsible "Uncle" Tim, even though you walked out on him you still expect him to

jump when you call, to look after the son you hauled
away from him because they were getting too close? My
God, what sort of a woman are you?'

Fern's lips parted with shock, and the colour drained
from her face. 'What...what do you mean?'

Suddenly it hit her—the way he so odiously spat out
the 'Uncle' Tim. Her shock and fury at what he believed
spun her head till she could hardly hang on to her senses.

'You evil-thinking bastard!' she seethed. 'How dare
you? How dare you speak to me like that?'

His anger was there too, just on the surface of the
grim set of his jaw. She wanted to strike out at it, to
slap it from his face for even considering being angry
with her. With a will of its own her free hand came up
and went to hit him hard, but he caught her wrist before
she got anywhere near his face. The shock of his grip
on her jarred the glass out of her other hand, and it
shattered into the fireplace. She felt the ice-cold liquid
splash against her legs, and it was all she needed to explode the tension inside her. This final insult and indignity was the last horror to end the worst day of her
life.

With a sob of anguish she wrenched away from him,
her eyes stinging with tears. 'I hate you for that!' she
croaked, the lump in her throat so huge and painful that
she could hardly get the words out. 'Tim...Tim...*is*
Charley's uncle...his real uncle...my brother...my very
own brother!'

The room swam and she tried to lurch away from him,
to run from the room and grab her son and
run...run...run!

He was still gripping her wrist, and she heard a clink
as he settled his glass on the mantelpiece, and then he

pulled her into his arms and with a ragged moan he held her tight against him. The terror of her discovery when she'd returned home and the relief of finding her son safe was too much, and now this . . . these wickedly cruel accusations from this man. She felt she had been struck by some fatal disease and had only minutes to live.

She fought him, only for a few desperate seconds, and then his soft murmurs of apology had her collapsing weakly against his chest.

Her sobs were the only sound in the room, his soft caresses on her tousled hair the only movement. Time stood still; there was no past, no future, just this warmth and comfort now. She cried and felt his arms tighten around her and then he eased his grip and lowered his head to her face to ease away her tears with the balm of his lips.

Then his lips reached her mouth, and her lips were parted, and the coming together of them was inevitable. Only one small sob hiccuped in her throat, not a protest but a sob of need. She clung to him and felt the warmth and the passion diffuse through her whole body. His tongue caressing the inner sweetness of her mouth urged her to forgive him for his veiled accusations. Something deep inside her argued that they had been born out of some sort of caring for her, and though the thought was flimsy and insubstantial she clung to it, desperately hopefully.

At last his mouth parted from hers and he looked down on her, and the anger had gone. His face, though still etched with worry, was not accusing any more.

'Forgive me, Fern,' he whispered softly. 'Forgive me, though it was unforgivable.'

Fern's eyes were still glazed with tears as she gazed up at him. She realised that his body, though hard against hers, was trembling very slightly. She realised hers was too, small tremors running through her body in warning. In that precious second she felt something had started between them, something she didn't want to acknowledge because it was so frightening.

'I think we both need another drink.' He drew back from her and she felt the loss of warmth and comfort and wished she wasn't quite so sensitive. 'Sit down; you look exhausted.'

Suddenly she was. She slumped down into the nearest sofa. Her head was still swimmy and she leaned her head back and watched him cross the room to the drinks table behind the other sofa. He poured the drinks and then he came towards her and handed her one of them.

'I'm truly sorry for what I thought,' he said once again. He stood towering over her, and she wished he didn't, because it made her feel so small and ineffectual against him. She knew then the danger she was in—not a physical danger, but one of the heart. She had been toying with fantasies since meeting him; nothing wrong with that, but now those fantasies were beginning to materialise into life, and she didn't want that, no, not yet.

'You weren't to know,' she uttered drily. She felt her strength returning slowly, a new strength, one that he wouldn't be able to sap so easily again. Fresh embarrassment swamped her for being so weak and clingy when he had comforted her, but she dismissed it abruptly. She had fooled herself into thinking he had kissed her because he couldn't resist her, but that wasn't the truth at all. She had put him into that position, and how else could he react but to feel sorry for her? But he had taken advantage, and she couldn't take that. 'But I think a further apology is necessary for what you just did to me,' she forced out bitterly.

His brow darkened. 'I don't know what you mean.'

Fern laughed cynically. 'You know exactly what I mean. I don't like being kissed that way.'

'And what is "that way"?'

'Taking advantage.'

'Well, that's a relief.' He half smiled. 'I'm glad you didn't accuse me of feeling sorry for you.'

'It all boils down to the same thing.'

'Hardly.'

'Hardly?' she repeated. 'What else could it be? Oh, I forgot, yes, you did say that you fancied me, and as I was traumatised by your unfounded accusations why not swoop in when my defences were down? You're nothing but an opportunist.'

'It wasn't that way at all. It seemed the right thing to do in the circumstances. You needed comforting and I wanted to comfort you, and let me stress that comfort doesn't stand for sympathy.'

'Very nearly,' she argued.

He shrugged. 'I'm not going to argue with you over something so trifling, but next time I kiss you I'll pick a more suitable time.'

'Your timing will never be right,' she told him bluntly and swallowed some more of her drink.

'Why?'

She glared up at him. Why did he insist on asking her *why* every time she refused him?

'Perhaps I'm not getting through to you. I'm not interested in an affair with you, and before you ask why I'll tell you...' So what was she going to say—that she

knew about him and Rachel? She hadn't quite the nerve
for that. 'I . . . I don't do affairs,' she told him in a soft
voice.

He raised his brows. 'Really?' he said silkily. 'I wasn't
aware I had suggested one.'

Fern felt the heat again, from him, the drink and the
fire. Bravely she stemmed yet another flush of embarrassment. 'You've kissed me and suggested taking me
out to dinner . . .'

'That constitutes an affair, does it? Funny little world
you live in.' He loosened his waistcoat and sat down on
the sofa across from her.

'It suggests an affair, James Causton,' she rallied.
'Dinner, a couple of kisses and an admission that you
fancy me; that adds up to an affair.'

He smiled, a thin smile. 'It has progressed to an affair
on that skimpy evidence, has it? What about a one-night
stand? Have you forgotten that?'

This time there was no controlling the rush of heat to
her face. She went with it and sipped her drink. Yes, of
course, that was exactly what he was offering. He already
had the full-blown affair—with Rachel.

'That is even more disgusting, and I don't do them
either,' she murmured.

'I agree, they are. I don't do one-night stands either,
but surely there is a happy medium we can strike somewhere in between?'

He hadn't denied he did affairs, though, Fern thought
miserably. She noted that his eyes were glittering now.
He was mocking her, or something stronger, taking her
vulnerability and playing with it as a cat played with
a mouse.

'No happy medium,' she told him firmly. 'I'm not to be taken advantage of. I have a son to think of...'

'Why not think of yourself for a change? Supposing you didn't have that son and you weren't a widow and I'd kissed you and offered to take you out to dinner, would you still refuse?'

He held her eyes, awaiting her answer, and for the life of her Fern couldn't come up with one. She could use Rachel, but she was trying to disregard that for the moment, and she was also trying to disregard the fact that he was separated from his wife and had a child himself to consider. So would she go out with him if all those considerations weren't blocking the way? She knew in an instant that she would. But those considerations were there and they were very powerful, not to be dismissed.

'A hypothetical question like that isn't worth the breath of answering,' she replied flatly.

'So you will go through life forfeiting your own life for your son?'

'I'm not giving anything up for my son,' she retorted hotly.

'So you have no needs?'

She eyed him warily. 'Do you?' she countered harshly, immediately thinking that was a rather silly question when she knew what she knew.

'Indeed I have. I love Victoria, but it doesn't stop me—— '

'Yes, I know!' she interrupted derisively, rubbing her forehead and putting her unfinished drink down on the hearth next to her. 'You're a man, and in cases like this there is a world of difference between what a man wants and what a woman wants. You can walk out the door and indulge yourself any time you like, but I can't.'

'I see absolutely no difference whatsoever. I'm sure if you really wanted to you could get a sitter and——'

'Look, you really are missing the whole point,' Fern insisted. 'This is a moral issue. I'm not interested in going out to satisfy my "needs" as you put it. What sort of a life is that for my son? You yourself poured scorn on me, thinking that "Uncle" Tim was a lover. The very fact that you thought Charley was exposed to "uncles" contradicts everything you are trying to tell me.'

'I was hardly suggesting becoming an "uncle" to Charley——'

Fern immediately got to her feet. 'I wouldn't allow you to be an uncle to my dog, let alone to my son!'

Slowly he got to his feet and put his glass down on the mantelpiece. She could see that he was annoyed and controlling it beautifully. Pity she didn't have such control over her own emotions.

'You make some very valid points,' he said coldly, 'and I concede most of them, but I think you ought to know that one of the reasons that I was indeed scornful in the first place was simply concern for your son's welfare——'

'His welfare is my concern, not yours!' she interrupted harshly.

'Nevertheless, the child was left waiting for someone to pick him up from school and no one did——'

'All right!' Fern snapped. 'Don't you think I'm suffering for that? I'll have nightmares for the rest of my life!' Her eyes blazed defiantly, but then she calmed herself. She shouldn't be arguing with him like this, because if it wasn't for his daughter's nannny picking

Charley up... She shuddered at the thought of what might have happened. 'I'm... I'm sorry. I don't know what I would have done if Sara hadn't...' She bit her lip and raised her chin. 'I really am very grateful.'

He nodded but made no comment, and she hoped he'd believed her. 'You... you were saying... you said "one of the reasons"...'

He gave her a very small smile. 'The other reason doesn't matter now.' He bent down and picked up her glass, and with his own from the mantelpiece he took them over to the drinks table.

'I... I don't want another drink——'

'I wasn't going to offer it. I'll drive you home.'

'I'll drive myself home, thank you,' she told him abrasively. This man could take over her life if she wasn't careful.

'You've been drinking. That wouldn't be wise,' he clipped assertively.

Dear God, now he was adding driving under the influence to her failings. Most of the drink was in the hearth anyway, but she didn't argue. What was the point? He thought her totally irresponsible, whatever she might say. She kneaded her forehead and wished the day had never happened. She felt such a fool, such a bad mother.

'Could... could you ring for a taxi, then...?'

'It isn't necessary——'

'It is!' Fern insisted, suddenly angry with him now, born out of her own inadeqacies *and* something else. 'You should practise what you preach, James Causton. You've been drinking too.'

'Only dry ginger,' he informed her. 'I never drink and drive.'

He said it with such deliberation that it made Fern
wonder if he'd had a brush with the law, but more than
likely it was a holier-than-thou attitude which threaded
through part of his life. No, the strait-laced, sophisticated James Causton wouldn't fall foul of anything but
the saddle of his horse and seducing rich, spoilt socialites.

'Annie has made up a bed for Charley——'

'No way!' Fern protested. Who on earth did he think
he was, taking over her and Charley's life like this?

James Causton shrugged, picked up the internal
phone, and spoke to Sara, asking her to bring Charley
down, as he wouldn't be staying the night after all.

He turned to her. 'Victoria suggested he stayed all night
as soon as they got home, and as we didn't know when
you would be back nothing more was said.'

Guilt swamped Fern once again. This was all so hor-
ribly uncomfortable. 'I'm sorry; thank you,' she
murmured.

Charley didn't thank her, though, when they stepped
out into the hall. Her son and Victoria came bounding
down the stairs, with Sara following a bit more sedately,
but only just. Charley wasn't very happy.

'Oh, Mummy! I wanted to stay——'

'Yes, please, Fern, let Charley——'

Charley swung on Victoria and gave her a push. 'She's
Mummy, not Fern!' Charley cried.

'Well, she's not *my* mummy!' Victoria screeched.

'That's enough, you two.'

As always, Sara was there to calm everyone down.
Fern noticed that James Causton looked quite non-
plussed by the two children squabbling after they had
looked so happy earlier. She thought that perhaps he
hadn't much insight into the erratic behaviour of

children. But fathers like him usually left the bringing-up of children to nannies.

'I can call you Fern, can't I?' the small girl appealed to Fern. 'I can't call you "Aunty", because you're not.'

To Fern's surprise the girl slipped her small hand into hers. Fern took the gesture as one to gather support from her against Charley. How devious the child was. Charley was quick to notice too and took Fern's other hand. If he couldn't win, at least he could even the odds.

James cleared his throat. 'You could try Mrs McKay.'

'You don't call her that!' the child retorted and beamed up at Fern, this time looking for support against her father.

'I'm sure Fern doesn't mind being called by her Christian name,' Sara intervened. 'Then Charley can call your daddy "James".'

Victoria looked uncertain about that for a second, then she let go of Fern's hand and ran to her father, pulling at his suit sleeve. 'Charley hasn't got a daddy...' Fern tensed and tightened her grip on her son's hand, anticipating something wicked and cruel coming from the unpredictable pink lips of the girl. 'And I haven't got a mummy and——'

'And it's time Charley was going,' Sara interrupted, stepping forward to give Charley a hug.

The hall seemed to heave a sigh of relief at Sara's intervention. Given that Victoria was very preoccupied with reproduction, it seemed the interruption came just in time.

'I'm just running Fern and Charley home,' James said to no one in particular.

'I want to come,' Victoria whined. 'I want to see Sacha.'

'You can wait till the weekend. Would you like to bring Charley up on Saturday or Sunday?' Sara asked, going over James Causton's head, Fern immediately thought.

James Causton thought the same thing and voiced it. 'Since when have you taken the role of mistress of this house, Sara?'

Fern felt embarrassment flooding her once again. It was quite obvious he didn't want them anywhere near his property again.

Sara grinned. 'You'll be in Brussels, James. Honestly, I and your secretary know more about what you are doing than you do.'

James raked a hand through his dark hair. 'Yes, I'd forgotten,' he uttered.

'Why don't you bring Victoria down to the cottage instead?' Fern suggested. It was the least she could offer Sara in return for her thoughtfulness today; besides, she liked her very much and she'd been short on female friends these last years. 'Then Sacha won't get into any trouble,' she added caustically for James Causton's benefit.

'Lovely!' Sara enthused, and Victoria gave a skip of excitement. 'I'll phone you to make the final arrangements. Victoria has just started ballet lessons on Saturdays and I'll have to check her times.'

'Thanks for looking after Charley so well,' Fern called back as they went out of the front door.

The cottage was ablaze with light when James halted the Land Rover in the lane minutes later.

'Uncle Tim's here!' Charley cried as he sighted his uncle's car parked by the side of the cottage. Before he could leap out of the Land Rover Tim was out of the front door and running towards them.

'Fern are you all right? Good God, whatever happened?'

Charley leapt out and flung himself at Tim, who gathered him into his arms.

'Thank God you're safe.' He picked the boy up and Charley clung to him.

Fern jumped out and James Causton stayed in the driving seat.

'This...this is my neighbour...' she started to explain.

Suddenly Tim let out a groan. 'Look, you'd better come inside. I have to call the police again. Hopefully I can catch them before they get here, though they're probably on their way. I called them when I got over here and found the house empty, all the lights on and your car gone...' He started to run back to the cottage with Charley in his arms.

'Oh, no!' Fern breathed, the weight of the whole terrible day dragging her down till she could barely put one foot in front of the other. Now there were going to be squad cars all over the place, and as if she hadn't been punished enough she was going to get stick from the law for wasting valuable police time.

'It's just one of those days,' James sighed as he got out of the Land Rover. He came round to her side of the car and slid his arm comfortingly around her shoulder, and she leaned into him because she felt so sick and weak.

That was the way they walked into the cottage and that was the way they were when Rachel greeted them in the small hallway of Fern's home.

CHAPTER FOUR

TRAUMATISED as she was, Fern could still register the
look of disbelief in Rachel's eyes. No concern for
Charley, Fern bitterly thought, just that stunned look
of disbelief and then her eyes flashing warily at the grip
James had on her shoulders.

Because of the limited space in the hall Fern quickly
pulled away from James's comforting support and
stumbled past her brother, who was copiously offering
apologies down the phone, past Rachel, who was stiff
with repressed aggression, and into the warm kitchen,
where Charley was sprawled with Sacha on the rug,
hugging her tightly.

Fern turned to see that James had followed her into
the kitchen. His face was infused with a dark colour that
Fern could only assume was brought on by sheer embarrassment at coming face to face with his mistress in
probably the last place on earth he thought he would
run into her.

Rachel followed meekly and for once did something
that mildly surprised Fern. She went to the Aga, snatched
up the kettle, and started to fill it noisily at the sink.

Tim came into the kitchen and opened his mouth to
explain, and Fern immediately came to her senses.

'Not now, Tim,' she ordered sharply, frowning and
indicating with a nod of her head her son, now kneeling
beside Sacha, tickling her tummy with wide-eyed inno-

cence. 'Charley, take Sacha up with you and get ready for bed...'

'Will you come and read me a story, Uncle Tim?'

'Of course, Charley-boy. I'll be up in a minute.'

Charley scampered up from the floor and to every-one's surprise went straight up to James, who had no choice but to stoop down to the boy as he stretched up to put his arms around his neck. 'You won't forget your promise, will you? I've never touched a baby lamb before.' He kissed James briefly on the cheek, and Fern watched in astonishment and wondered what had gone on in the time before she had arrived at Bourne Hall to pick Charley up.

'No, I won't forget, Charley,' he said quietly, ruffling the boy's hair.

The silence and the atmosphere in the warm kitchen was edible. Fern could taste it. Her eyes flickered to Rachel, who was watching the whole scene with in-credulous red parted lips. In spite of the trauma of the night she still looked amazingly well turned out, her make-up perfect, her hair coiled seductively around her face, and her designer clothes hanging on her perfect figure as if this was their first airing. In sharp contrast, Fern felt like the rug out in the hall that Sacha had savaged in her loneliness.

For once Fern was glad Charley forgot manners and ran up the stairs without saying goodnight to Rachel. In that moment Fern almost loathed her, because if it weren't for Tim giving her extra coaching outside office hours none of them would be standing here taking ten-tative glances at each other. But that wasn't fair, Fern immediately thought guiltily. It wasn't anyone's fault this had happened but her own.

Fern took a breath. 'This is my brother, Tim,' she directed to James. 'James Causton, my neighbour. His...his...' Oh, heavens, did Rachel know that her lover had a daughter? If she didn't she was about to, because Fern had to offer some sort of explanation. 'His daughter, Victoria, goes to the same school as Charley, and Sara, her nanny, took Charley back with her to Bourne Hall when you didn't turn up.'

All the time Fern was speaking her dark brown eyes switched from Rachel to James. Rachel didn't know; her face paled and then her mouth thinned. James remained icily composed, a state he'd induced after the departure of Charley, which told Fern a lot about his relationship with Rachel. Victoria wasn't a consideration in it!

Her heart went to neither of them but tore for her brother at this moment. She noticed how drawn and pale he looked and she guessed it was because of Charley.

Tim shook James's hand warmly, though the uplifting of James's hand was hesitant, as if he wasn't sure whether he should like him or not after this awful night which was brought about by Tim's incompetence.

'I don't know what to say, James,' Tim started. '"Pleased to meet you" seems a bit inadequate at this juncture. I can't tell you how badly I feel about all this——'

'Don't feel bad, Tim,' Rachel cut in so sharply that all eyes were suddenly upon her. 'Charley *isn't* your responsibility. None of this is your fault. Fern should have——'

'Just a minute!' Fern suddenly blazed. She wasn't going to take that, not when it was so obviously said to discredit her in James Causton's eyes. Her heart thudded so violently that she felt sick with the pain of all this. Her whole being was diminishing by the minute.

'Hold on, Rachel . . .' Tim interrupted. 'Sorry, James, this is my partner's daughter, Rachel Edwards. She's joining the company shortly and we were going over some paperwork tonight and got so involved...' He didn't finish because guilt swamped him and there was really no excuse for what he had done.

'Yes, we have met,' simpered Rachel, not particularly to Tim. 'Daddy and James are old friends.'

Fern felt sure that was added for her benefit, almost a boastful statement that her father's connection with James was far more important and binding. But surely if James and Robert Edwards were indeed old friends Rachel would know about Victoria and James's past, about the wife who was conspicuous by her absence? Fern had the distinct feeling she didn't know. Curious.

'I must apologise on behalf of Fern, James,' Rachel knifed on. 'You look as if you're hating all this fuss, and I can't say I blame you. How thoughtless of Fern to involve you in her trifling domestic business.'

'I assure you there is nothing trifling about the welfare of Fern's son, Rachel,' James cut in stiffly, giving Tim such a piercing look that even Fern felt for her brother. 'It was the least I could do and I was happy to be involved. I'm just delighted that Charley came to no harm. Now if you will excuse me...' He turned to Fern. 'I'll have your car sent down to you in the morning.' Then he walked out of the kitchen, and the silence was only broken by the front door slamming shut.

Only then did Fern move to slump down in the chair by the Aga. Her whole body had been as stiff as a rod of iron while all that had been going on; now she was as weak as a bowl of strawberry jelly and twice as ineffectual.

'Fern, I'm really sorry.' Tim squatted down beside her. 'I'll never forgive myself for this—never.' The grating emotion in his voice was testimony to how deeply sorry he felt.

As Fern expected, Rachel no longer felt inclined to argue that Tim wasn't to blame now that James wasn't here. She no longer felt inclined to finish making the tea either; the kettle hissed warningly on the hob. Wearily Fern got to her feet and rescued it, sliding it to the edge of the hob.

'It was terrible, Tim,' she told him quietly. 'I was frantic when I got back...' Her voice trailed and she cleared her throat. 'The worst thing of all was imagining what was going through Charley's mind as he waited for you. Oh, Tim,' Fern breathed emotionally, her eyes wide and tearful. 'How could you?'

Tim bowed his head remorsefully for a second, and Fern imagined what he must have gone through when she had phoned. All her emotions went out to him then and she touched the top of his head and let out a breathy sigh. This was all her fault. Tim had a business to run and he'd done enough in the past to help her. She was being selfish. 'Let's forget it, Tim,' she whispered. 'Charley didn't even realise what was going on. Thank heavens for Sara. I don't want to fall out with you over this...'

'But I deserve it, sis,' Tim mourned regretfully, getting to his feet, then slipping his arm around her shoulder and hugging her. 'You know how I feel about you and Charley. I wouldn't intentionally let either of you down... It's just that... well, Rachel's off to Brussels this weekend and we wanted to get this work cleared up before...'

Fern iced up inside at the mention of Brussels, and her whole body stiffened. Just then Charley called out, and Fern's eyes brimmed with fresh tears. She turned her face to see Tim's torment, and her heart went out to him.

'You... you'd better go up and read Charley a quick story...'

Tim nodded and kissed her forehead before going upstairs.

Sure that he was out of earshot, Fern steeled herself to face Rachel. She was standing by the sink, out of place in Fern's domesticity, out of place in her life. She was totally unaffected by everything that had happened. She couldn't even show any concern for Charley, let alone for what Tim must have gone through.

'And how dare you try and put me down in James Causton's eyes?' Fern flamed at her. Never would she let her know what she knew about her and James—that would do no one any good—but she wasn't going to be made a fool of in her own home. 'It's thanks to him and his daughter's nanny that no harm came to my son——'

'Your son,' Rachel spat contemptuously. 'The bloody child is expected to be everyone's centre of the universe. He's your child, Fern, not Tim's or James Causton's. In future you look after him. Tim's always put you before the business——'

'That's not true!' Fern protested, a hot flush of anger whirling through her.

'It's nothing but the truth,' Rachel fired back sarcastically. 'Tim had work to do tonight; he was helping me, and that is far more important than having to pick up your son from school, and, as for James's involvement, what a position to put the poor man in——'

'What the devil is going on down here?' Tim stormed from the stairway. 'I can't hear myself speak up here.'

Rachel flushed hotly and snatched at her shoulder-bag lying on the work surface. She waited till Tim had returned to Charley's bedroom before releasing some more harsh words, this time in a hushed whisper. 'I've known James Causton for a long time, Fern, and I can tell you this isn't his scene, looking out for poor widows and snotty-nosed kids. You put him in an embarrassing situation tonight. Couldn't you see how he was hating it all? No, I don't suppose you could, because all you ever think about is your precious son.' She thrust the strap of her bag over her shoulder and gave Fern one last spiteful glare. 'Tell Tim I'm going to wait in the car and not to be long.'

With an exaggerated huff Rachel stormed out of the kitchen as James had done earlier, and Fern just covered her face with her hands, her whole body shaking from head to toe. Now she really did hate Rachel for exposing the truth. That wretched truth hurt.

Tim came down the stairs, stood in front of her, and folded his arms around her. 'You've had a terrible night,' he husked gruffly as he stroked her hair in a desperate attempt to comfort her.

'So have you,' she managed to utter weakly. 'I'm sorry, Tim. I'm really sorry. I...I shouldn't put these demands on you.' She lifted her flushed face and tried to smile for her brother, to reassure him that she was all right. But it was hard, because so many issues tonight had been brought out into the open, and they didn't sit well on top of Fern's already weighty emotions. 'Rachel's waiting in the car,' she told him. 'I'll read to Charley...'

'He's almost asleep anyway,' Tim breathed. He lifted her chin and smiled down at her. 'I'll call you tomorrow. I'm really sorry for tonight, for everything.'

Fern nodded, accepting his apologies because she knew they were genuine. He'd suffered too, she knew.

'That Causton...' He paused as he widened his grin. 'He's a nice guy.' He kissed her forehead and let her go.

He's not a nice guy at all, Fern mused as she shut the front door after him. He's off to Brussels this weekend with Rachel, and the rotten pair of them deserve each other!

Charley was already asleep by the time she stepped into his bedroom. Sacha was curled on a rug at the foot of his bed, the two pals united in exhaustion. Fern bent down and kissed her son's warm cheek. He *was* the centre of her universe.

Fern went to her bedroom, kicked off her shoes, and slowly peeled off her clothes. The temptation to crawl into bed and pull the covers over her head forever was almost succumbed to but she fought it off. She wanted to think. She slid into her towelling dressing-gown and went downstairs to make some tea.

A primeval need for comfort urged her to light the log fire in the cosy sitting-room. It was warm enough with the background central heating, but she needed a living flame to soothe away the effects of the terrible night. Her thoughts tumbled around her head; the 'if only's crashed around till she let out a mournful plea to be released from it all.

It was all her fault and the sooner she accepted it the better it would be for her comfort. Rachel, she regretfully admitted, was right. She wasn't James Causton's scene. What a complex character he was. Tonight he had shown derision, compassion, even plain old passion, and then in front of his mistress had defended her. That had really confused her. But she wasn't going to be confused any more. She was going to steer very clear of him in future. She had been attracted to him; that she could readily admit to herself, because now there was no danger. One day she would find space in her heart for someone else, but not for him. James Causton was as out of bounds in her heart as Sacha was in his precious barns.

'No, Charley, James didn't mean today,' Fern told her son firmly as they drove past Bourne Hall after school the next day.

Her car had been delivered back to the cottage in the very early hours of the morning. Fern had heard the engine of the Metro and leapt out of bed, only to see a young man she had never seen before parking the car by the cottage and taking a short cut across her garden to the Hall beyond the meadow. Had she honestly expected James Causton to bring it back?

'I expect Victoria will let you know when the lambs come,' Fern added, 'and then you can go up and see them.'

Charley was placated for the moment, but for how long? Fern wondered. She had vowed to keep away from James, but that wasn't going to be easy with the friendship Charley and Victoria had forged. A difficult one, this. She liked Sara too and would like her friendship, but that would mean possible contact with her employer, and that was to be avoided like a community virus.

'Get changed before you go out into the garden with Sacha,' Fern called out as Charley burst into the cottage ahead of her.

Fern slid out of her jacket and went through to the kitchen. The first sight that hit her was the vase of spring flowers on the kitchen table, and she had to smile, though the flowers were hardly amusing. They had arrived when she had returned from dropping Charley off at school that morning.

Fern adjusted them and bent her head to inhale the deep scent of the freesias. She should have binned them as soon as they arrived, but flowers were flowers and didn't deserve such an indignity. Her heart had raced when they had arrived and she had torn at the envelope that accompanied them, thinking that they were from James; heavens, she had actually *hoped* they were from him! It had been a crazy thought after her soul-searching the night before; nevertheless, the disappointment had bitten deep when she had read the card from Rachel, apologising for her wicked outburst the night before.

Like hell she was sorry, Fern uncharitably thought, but had to laugh. She could see exactly which way Rachel's devious mind had worked. James Causton had brought her and Charley home last night and that must have been a revelation for the woman, especially as he had shown such care for her, his arm comfortingly tucked around her shoulders, and that defence of her and Charley and his obvious irritation at Rachel's unsympathetic attitude to the trauma they had all been through.

No, Rachel didn't want to fall out with Fern, not when her closest neighbour was her lover.

Besides—Fern grinned as she moved the vase a few inches to the right—these placatory flowers were a symbol of Rachel's jealousy, and there was a certain satisfaction in that, not in a spiteful way, but it was nice to think someone actually thought her capable of being a threat where affairs of the heart were concerned.

'Char—— Oh!' Fern took an instinctive step back from the back door, where she was about to call Charley in for his tea.

'Sorry, did I make you jump?'

'Yes,' Fern murmured, staring up at James Causton. No city clothes today. Her heart raced to think that the lambs might have started to arrive and he'd come for Charley. She looked past him.

'They've gone tearing down to that old barn of yours with Sacha. Is it safe for them?'

'You brought Victoria? Yes...yes...it's quite safe. It's the log barn and Charley has taken it over, built himself a camp in there.' She stepped back. 'You...you'd better come in.'

'I came to see if you were all right after yesterday. You went through quite a trauma and I was worried about you.'

Oh, no, this she didn't need. Not kindness and concern from him. She stood with her back to Rachel's flowers and leaned on the edge of the table. She felt suddenly hostile towards him, doubting whether he had come to ask after her welfare. Perhaps he thought Rachel might have confided in her about their affair and he wanted her to keep quiet about it... A divorce pending, maybe...a messy one.

'Thank you for your concern. As you can see, life goes on,' she said tightly.

He frowned slightly at her abrasive attitude, but made no comment. He moved to warm his hands at the Aga and then turned to face her, plunging his hands into the pockets of his jeans as he did it. To Fern's suspicious mind the expectant stance was a give-away, as was the way his eyes looked deeply into hers. Fern knew what he was looking for; some sign of what she knew.

'What exactly are you here for, James?' she managed to ask.

'I thought I'd just told you—concern for you.' He looked puzzled.

Fern smiled wryly. 'Concern for me? I wish it were that simple.'

He frowned again, dark brows bunching. 'What do you mean?'

'After last night I think that is quite obvious and would be to a cross-eyed monkey. Don't come here with your curiosity packaged as concern. You want to know what I know, and you might as well know that I know it all!'

His mouth softened into half a smile. 'I wish I *knew* what you were gabbling on about.'

'Ha! As if you *didn't* know!'

'Please, Fern——'

'Rachel!' Fern exploded.

He sighed. 'Well, I'm certainly glad that is out. Rachel, is it? You obviously have something on your mind, so out with the rest of it.'

'No! You out with the rest of it. It has absolutely nothing to do with me. I'm just a very unwilling onlooker.'

'I'd say you were in it up to your pretty little neck.'

Fern's eyes widened in surprise at that. 'I fail to see what I have to do with your private life.'

'I agree. You have nothing to do with my private life, yet, but I must admit it came as quite a surprise to me that you run with the Rachel Edwards brat pack.'

'I run with no one, James,' she told him haughtily. 'I know Rachel through my brother and his partnership with her father, but we aren't friends, I assure you.'

'I'm glad to hear that.'

'I'm sure you are. But don't feel too safe. I'm not her confidante, but I know what I know...'

James sighed wearily. 'Here we go again.'

'Yes, here we go again,' Fern retorted bitterly. 'You know, last night I was quite flattered you stuck up for me and Charley in front of Rachel, but now I think I'm beginning to see the reason why.'

'And what reason is that?' he asked directly. 'I'd be very interested to hear it.'

Suddenly she was unsure of just about everything. 'I...I...well...you were...you might need me...as some sort of a go-between as I live so close to you... I mean, you wouldn't want it common knowledge...not...not if you have a...have a divorce coming up.'

Her accusations hung in the air. Slowly James Causton took his hands out of his pockets. He lowered his head for a second and drew both hands through his hair before looking at her again. When he spoke his voice was so soft that Fern only just caught it. 'What exactly has she told you?'

Fern stared at him, feeling oddly unsettled that he had done or said nothing to defend himself. She had expected something, some sort of a denial of the affair, for the simple reason that he had asked her out, kissed her a couple of times, and admitted that he fancied her like hell, so, being a damned womaniser, he would deny an affair with someone else, wouldn't he? Shouldn't he?

'I've told you, we aren't close friends,' she whispered hoarsely. She gave a small laugh. 'Yes, I suppose you think we are. Knowing your warped sense of justice I bet you think I'm in on all this and willing to be another of your conquests. After all, last night you thought me cheap enough to have a succession of "uncles" for Charley——'

Suddenly he was angry and stepped towards her. Fern stepped back and round the table to put it between them both.

He stopped. 'I've apologised for that misjudgement of character,' he argued strongly. 'My only excuse was that we hardly knew each other.'

'But now I know a helluva lot more about you, James Causton, and what I know doesn't smell very sweet! How dare you try and seduce me while you are already having an——?'

Suddenly the two children and Sacha burst into the kitchen.

'Can I show Victoria my computer games?' Without waiting for a reply, Charley threw off his jacket and flew up the stairs, Victoria and Sacha following at the same breakneck speed.

James eyed her coldly across the table. It was as if he hadn't noticed the passing of the children.

'You were saying...' he urged darkly.

'I don't believe you!' Fern breathed in exasperation, sweeping her hair back from her forehead. 'You know exactly what I'm saying!'

There was a deathly hush then, not even a sound from the children upstairs. James Causton didn't move, but for a throb of a nerve at his temple.

So he was angry, and he had no right to be. Fern waited and waited for him to say or do something. She watched his face all the time, looking for signs of remorse, defiance, anything. It was obvious that he wasn't going to apologise for taking her for a fool. 'Sorry' wasn't a word in his vocabulary, remorse not a feeling he knew about.

She was the first to speak. 'As I suspected,' she hissed. 'You haven't a thought for anyone but yourself.' She shook her head in disbelief. 'You know, I made a bad character judgement too. For one atom of a second I liked you; even knowing what I knew about you and Rachel, I was prepared to give you the benefit of the doubt. But there isn't any doubt now. You can't even deny it, which I suppose is to your credit. It would be ten times worse if you did deny your affair with Rachel now.'

Another great empty silence in which Fern snuggled her thoughts together. Right from the very moment of meeting him she had known he was seeing Rachel, and yet she had allowed herself to be attracted to him; she had controlled it, but nevertheless she had allowed a few fantasies. But it was that great put-down by Rachel the previous night that was causing all this misery and anger now. She wasn't even angry with him, just with herself for cheating herself into thinking he might care.

He spoke at last, flatly, unemotionally, as if he wondered what he was doing here anyway.

'So Rachel and I are having an affair, are we? So if she didn't confide in you, how did you know what was going on?'

'Does it matter?' she bleated painfully.

'Yes, it damned well matters! Because if you know others might too.'

'Of course, you don't want any trouble, do you? Squire of the bloody green belt——'

'Stop this, Fern!' he ordered through thinned lips. His voice was barely a harsh whisper; nevertheless, it locked Fern's tirade in her throat. 'I repeat—how did you know about Rachel and me?'

Fern licked her dry lips before speaking. 'I saw you together...'

'When?'

'I don't know when!' she blurted irritably. 'Months ago, before I moved here, in a wine bar in Guildford...'

'The start of it all,' James breathed anxiously, moving back from the table and raking a hand through his hair once again. He turned away from her, moved back to the Aga, then turned to face her again. 'And on the strength of that you presume we are having an affair?' he suggested gravely. 'Two people of opposite sexes having lunch together and you assume an affair?'

'If it were only that, no, I wouldn't,' Fern answered him honestly. For some reason her stomach was slowly knotting, and it was because of his show of anxiety. She didn't understand that. 'At the time I didn't know you, didn't know who you were.' She steeled herself and raised her chin. 'OK, it could have been an innocent lunch date, even a business lunch. I'll accept that, but what I won't accept is any excuse for the second time I saw you together——'

'The second time?' he asked in disbelief, as if he suspected she had followed them.

Why was she feeling so uncomfortable about this? It was awful, dragging all his sordid love life out in to the open, and for what? It really was no concern of hers.

'In a lay-by,' Fern admitted triumphantly. 'And by no stretch of the imagination can that be passed off as a business meeting. Bumper to bumper in a lonely lane? Wrapped lovingly in each other's arms? Kissing passionately as if the world were coming to an end? That stinks of only one sort of business—monkey business—and that only means one thing, James Causton. You have something to hide!'

His raised brows reached for the sky. 'Any more sightings?' he asked sarcastically. 'I'm beginning to think I'm getting more attention than a peregrine falcon in my own back yard!'

'N-no. I think two is enough, more than enough,' she told him tightly.

His dark brows lowered over accusing eyes. 'Two is enough to establish an affair, is it? I have a vague feeling we have touched on this subject before, you ten paces ahead of me as usual. You did say girls were more advanced than boys, but this is ridiculous.'

'Yes, but we're not talking about children here,' Fern seethed, despising him for not owning up to the truth. 'We are talking about a very beautiful mature woman and a very good-looking——'

'Thanks for the compliment.'

'Don't try and side-track me. I don't accept that you are not having an affair with Rachel——'

'I haven't denied it yet.'

'Don't bother trying it——'

'But I will,' he cut back very sharply. 'I will deny it to the death.' His gleaming eyes confirmed that.

Fern parted her lips and then closed them again. She didn't know what to think now. She didn't even know if she believed him or not. Had she jumped to all these conclusions on the strength of two sightings of him with Rachel? Oh, but there was more, much more. That kiss in the car, for starters; perhaps if they hadn't been in such a give-away clinch she could be swayed, but she had seen it all and there was nothing wrong with her eyesight, and besides, she knew women, and Rachel definitely gave off vibes.

'Well, you've had plenty to say so far, so why not add that you believe me?' he challenged coldly.

Fern stayed mute, because she wasn't sure of anything. He was denying it and she wanted to believe him, but she'd seen the wretched evidence for herself.

At last he spoke. 'Silence is sometimes more revealing than anything, Fern,' he said flatly. 'It makes me wonder if there is more to this than meets the eye. Perhaps you are not quite so concerned for a *supposed* impending divorce. Could it be that you are more concerned for this *supposed* affair between me and Rachel because it might interfere with your own hopes in my direction?'

Fern took a sharp intake of breath and her heart spasmed so warningly that she felt quite faint. She tried to laugh the arrogant suggestion away, but her lips stayed frozen in a grimace of disbelief. She couldn't speak; whatever she said would only add to this agony he was putting her through anyway.

Jerkily she eased herself away from the table. Where was Charley when she needed him? Why couldn't he burst in——?

'Daddy, I want a computer like Charley's,' Victoria demanded as she hurtled down the stairs.

Thank heaven for little girls! Fern said to herself.

Charley and the faithful hound followed in hot pursuit and they all vied for James's attention, Victoria demanding, Charley backing her, and Sacha pawing at his corded jeans as if she'd been programmed to back her as well.

James Causton was still making excuses as he helped Victoria into the Land Rover.

'I bet she gets one,' Charley shouted to Sacha as they tore back upstairs. 'Mummy,' he called over the banister, 'I like Victoria. Do you like her daddy?'

'I . . . yes, of course,' Fern lied for a quiet life.

'Great!' he called back and ran up the rest of the stairs.

Yes, just great, Fern mused with a frown as she set the table for tea, wondering what ideas that forward little girl was putting into Charley's mind.

And what ideas was James Causton putting into her own? Could he have worried a small nerve with that suggestion of his that she was more concerned for herself than anyone? And had she lied to her own son when she had always taught him honesty was the best policy in life?

She didn't exactly hate James Causton; that was the only thing she was sure about for the moment. He had denied an affair with Rachel and she wanted to believe him, but she didn't know him very well, and perhaps she didn't know herself very well either, because she was letting it all matter.

CHAPTER FIVE

FERN could hardly believe her luck. She had deliberated so long and hard over her little ploy—a ploy she had developed to occupy her thoughts rather than dwell on James Causton—that she felt it would be doomed to disaster because of her hesitancy. All week she had toyed with the idea of a bit of matchmaking and wondered how she could accomplish it. Tim had given her the answer this very morning when he had phoned to suggest taking Charley out sledging for the afternoon to make up for forgetting to pick him up from school in the week.

Fern's idea was better: why not come over for tea and take two children and a nanny and a frisky dog sledging in James Causton's meadow, which had a perfect gentle slope ideal for bucketing children down? Would he mind? Tim had asked. He wasn't here, off on a trip to Brussels, Fern had told her brother, to which he had laughed and said what a coincidence, so were Rachel and her father. Some coincidence, Fern had inwardly seethed. But it was all fuel to the hatred she was now building up against her not so friendly neighbour.

She concentrated on her matchmaking ploy. Tim needed a woman in his life, and Fern liked Sara enormously, and they might fall hopelessly in love and someone in this cruel world might snatch at a bit of happiness. There was only one small hiccup in her life to deal with, and that wasn't much of a problem. All she had to do was tell herself that James Causton was a lying, arrogant creep a hundred times a day, and her personal problem was solved.

Fern grinned out of the cottage window, watching her brother and Sara and the children trudging through the snow, dragging the sledge behind them, and Sacha, of course, leaping excitedly at their heels. A thick fall of snow in the night had been an added bonus to her plans. To Fern there was something magically romantic about snow. It was beautiful and a perfect backdrop to a scenario of falling in love. Sara and Tim were getting along like a house on fire and Fern didn't feel one iota of guilt for her actions.

She drew back from the window, still smiling with self-satisfaction, and started preparing the tea. She'd already set the kitchen table for five. Annie had been a dear and sent down an enormous home-baked fruit cake, and Fern unwrapped it and placed it at the centre of the table. Keep going, girl, she told herself resolutely. You'll soon forget the Squire of Bourne Hall.

'How did you know I was coming?'

Fern nearly leapt a foot off the floor with fright. She swung round to the door of the back porch and gaped at James Causton, who was easing out of his snowy boots. Her mouth opened and shut like the valves of her heart.

'I . . . I didn't.'

'Five place settings.' He nodded at the table and then stepped into the room.

'Full marks for observation,' she rallied, her heart still pumping furiously. Why did the man have such an effect on her when she had repeated her lines faithfully since last he was here? 'T-Tim's here—my brother. He and Sara have taken the children sledging. Why aren't you in Brussels?' If he wasn't, and Rachel and her father were, then...then they couldn't have been going together. Coincidence? Stranger things had happened. But maybe she had pricked James Causton's conscience. Whatever, Fern felt a small wash of relief.

'I cancelled at the last minute. It was a low-key business meeting that wasn't very important. Can I give you a hand?'

Fern started to laugh softly, and James looked at her with concern.

'I'm quite domesticated, you know. I won't break anything... What are you laughing at?'

Fern turned away from him and opened a wall cupboard to get out the plates, grinning like a silly Cheshire cat as she did it.

'I'm just laughing with relief.' But she didn't tell him the source of the relief. She handed him another plate. 'Are you staying for tea?'

'That was the general idea. Am I welcome, though?'

'Yes, you're welcome,' she murmured, feeling incredibly shy for a second.

'Why the sudden change of heart? Last time I was here I was hardly flavour of the month.'

Fern watched him as he shifted the plates around the table, making room for his own. Later, when the children came in, they would all be gathered round that table and James would be there as well, and she wondered how she was going to feel about it. For so long she hadn't been a part of anyone, the other half of a pair...but she wasn't about to be one now, she thought wistfully. He was just a neighbour and Victoria's father, but...but he was here, not in Brussels with Rachel, and that was enough for the time being.

'Did you hear me?'

'Oh . . . sorry. I was miles away.' She took bread from the bread bin and started to make sandwiches. 'This is a kids' tea-party, you know,' she told him evasively. 'Nothing very sophisticated. Sandwiches and cake and some scones——'

'Why the change of heart, Fern?' he repeated, standing so close to her that she could feel his warmth.

Now, because she knew he wasn't having an affair with Rachel, or if he had been it was over, she didn't mind the awareness it aroused in her. It was quite a nice feeling and she allowed it to seep through her, tingling her nerve-endings. It was going nowhere, so she was safe with indulging it for a while.

She didn't look at him, just concentrated hard on spreading the slices of brown bread with butter. 'My accusations were unfounded,' she told him. 'Well, not exactly . . . after all, I did see you twice with Rachel, and once you were kissing her and . . .' Oh, it was useless. She couldn't put aside the evidence of her own eyes, but perhaps she could mist over it a bit. It could have been an impulsive kiss, one born out of a moment of madness, men's needs and all that. And she so wanted to believe him. 'It . . . it looked very suspicious . . . but . . . well, you denied it and I believe you.'

'You didn't believe me then, so why now?'

Fern bit her lower lip. 'I . . . I did believe you, but it . . . it was the other thing you said that upset me.'

'What was that?'

She paused from buttering bread and looked at him. 'Don't make me repeat it,' she uttered softly.

He nodded his dark head and gave her a small smile. 'Was it about your intentions in my direction?'

' "Hopes" was the word you used, not "intentions".
Neither of them are applicable anyway, and don't ask
me if I'm sure about that. I know what led you to think
that way. I'm on my own with Charley and people always
think that a young widow with a young child to bring
up is always on the look-out for someone to lighten the
load.' She shook her head. 'I've already told you I'm
self-sufficient.'

Fern started to spread a slice of the bread with cream
cheese and chopped chives. James stood beside her, ready
to place another slice on top.

'Self-sufficient money and careerwise, but what about
affairs of the heart?'

Fern smiled, sliced through the sandwich, and went
on to the next. 'I don't need that. We've already dis-
cussed it.' She paused and looked directly into his dark
brown eyes. 'And don't tell me you think otherwise on
the basis of that kiss the other night...'

'It was quite a kiss,' he said with humour.

'Yes, it was,' she admitted on a smile, 'and not the
yellow-brick road to anything more.' And as she said
that she thought it applied to the kiss she had witnessed
between him and Rachel as well. The thought gave her
a warm feeling inside.

James laughed. 'You're different from anyone else I've
met. You're open and you say what you feel. Quite a
rarity in a woman.'

'It isn't rare at all,' Fern protested. 'You just haven't
met the right sort of women.'

'Oh, and you're the right sort of woman for me,
are you?'

Fern laughed and shook her head. 'I wouldn't be so
presumptuous as to suggest such a thing. What I'm trying

to say is that I'm the way I am with you because I'm not in the running. I can afford to be open because I'm not looking for a man in my life.'

'And yet you were furious with me, thinking I was having an affair with another woman and yet making a play for you at the same time.'

'Yes, I was,' she admitted openly and smiled. 'Quite contrary of me really, but that's the way I am. One man, one woman. Yes, I was furious and offended too. That must sound very old-fashioned, but I'm not a promiscuous person.'

'It makes a pleasant change.'

That came out as a world-weary statement, and Fern imagined that he was probably plagued by loose women. For all she knew, he might have a few on the go at the moment. She felt a tug inside her at the thought. There she was spouting how she didn't need a man in her life, yet this one had certainly had an impact on her, and as she glanced at him thoughtfully she rejected the idea that he had a string of women. Like her he was responsible for a small child, but men were different. His needs couldn't be so easily quashed.

Fern finished the sandwiches and covered them in clingfilm while James washed his hands at the sink. Domesticated he thought he was, but he was as messy as the children where cream cheese was concerned.

'Would you like a tea or a coffee now?' she offered.

He was gazing out of the window, drying his hands and watching the children screaming with excitement in the snow as Tim and Sara dragged them around on the sledge.

'I'd rather be out there on that toboggan,' he mused.

Fern came to stand next to him. 'Really?' she murmured, and her eyes were sparkling as they looked at each other. 'What's stopping us?'

'Certainly not old age,' James muttered with a grin.

They dressed hurriedly, Fern almost bubbling over with excitement. She paused at the doorway as James ran on ahead, turning once to beckon her on. For a fleeting second she saw Ralph instead of James, and for that second her heart tore. Her gloved hand tightened around the edge of the door and she felt a surge of loss so deep and painful that it brought hot tears to the backs of her eyes. In the sloping meadow, beyond the broken wire fence, Charley, their son, was leaping up and down with excitement as Tim, with Sara wedged between his legs on the sledge, was preparing to hurtle down the slope.

'Oh, Ralph,' Fern moaned sadly, biting her lip. Then, swallowing hard, she pulled the door shut behind her, plunged her hands into her pockets, and with her head lowered against the flurries of fresh snow she ran after James.

'My turn now, Daddy!' Victoria shrieked, her face almost feverish with excitement. Strands of wet, bedraggled hair were sticking out from under her red bobble hat and her eyes were bright blue orbs, sparkling with anticipation as she pulled at her father's oiled jacket. Fern thought that her mother must be very beautiful. She obviously took after her mother, not having much of her father about her. She wondered how a woman could leave a child. She wondered if she ever visited her. She wondered what had gone wrong in their marriage.

'Come on, Charley, there's room for you too,' James urged, shifting back on the sledge, tugging Victoria close to him and making room for Charley between his legs.

Laughing, Tim and Sara gave them a push, and they were off, but not for long. They ground to a halt and Sara ran down to give them another hearty shove, Sacha barking excitedly at her heels.

Tim's arm crept around Fern's shoulders. 'I know what you're thinking,' he murmured. 'The last time I was up in Scotland with you and Ralph and Charley we did this—drove to the granite quarries...'

'Same sledge,' Fern reminded him, leaning into her brother for comfort.

'He wouldn't mind, you know.'

'Who wouldn't mind about what?' she queried, though she thought she had a good idea what he was hinting at.

'Ralph wouldn't mind...you and James.'

Fern sighed, not wanting to let the thought drag her down. 'I know he wouldn't; he was that sort of guy,' she murmured desolately, 'but...but there's nothing doing there...'

'Not what Sara thinks.'

'Oh, yes?' Fern teased with a grin as she drew away from him. And there was she thinking how clever she was being by acting as some modern-day Cupid with her brother and Sara.

'Oh, yes,' he insisted. 'James Causton shouldn't be here. He cancelled a business meeting for you this weekend...'

Fern swooped down and gathered a handful of snow and hurled it at him. They were soon both laughing as the snowball fight commenced; at the same time Fern's heart was thudding with the thought that James had done that for her. It couldn't be true, though—could it?

'Hey, you two, grow up, will you?' Sara called with a laugh as she joined in.

'Your turn now, Mummy,' Charley called as they panted up the hill, James dragging the sledge behind him, Sacha bounding at his side.

'Daddy tipped us up in the snow,' Victoria wailed. 'I've got snow down my neck and Charley's got snow in his boots.'

'And you're both blue with cold,' Sara said with concern. 'I think you've had enough——'

'Mummy hasn't had her turn yet!' Charley protested valiantly.

'Daddy will take her!' Victoria screeched.

Fern caught James's eye and immediately looked away. She flushed with embarrassment at his pushy daughter.

'Great idea,' Sara enthused, throwing a knowing look towards Tim which Fern intercepted before it reached its target. 'Come on, Victoria and Charley, we'll go back to the cottage and get washed.'

'No!' the children chorused, fidgeting their feet in the impacted snow.

'We want to watch,' Victoria giggled. 'Daddy might roll Fern in the snow.'

'Indeed he might,' James grated with humour as he steadied the sledge and sat on it.

'And my mummy might roll James in the snow!' Charley blurted at Victoria, his attempt at one-upmanship.

'Indeed she won't!' Fern laughed, knowing she wasn't going to be able to get out of it, and did she really want to? Bravely she stepped between James's booted feet and lowered herself between his legs. His arms folded around her to grasp at the rope that was supposed to act as steering but never did.

'Ready?' James breathed into the back of her neck, and his warm breath on her skin between her scarf and her jacket sent a small shiver down her back.

Fern nodded, and suddenly they were jolted forward by an army of well-wishers. Fern clung on to James's knees and leaned back into him as the wind beat against her face. The two adults' weight had the sledge powering down the now icy slope in no time. The excited cries of the children grew more distant; Sacha had long since given up the chase.

The wind rushed in Fern's ears as the sledge careered on and on; her stomach was in the region of her throat, her eyes narrowed against the cold. They had gone beyond where the others had gone, ploughing through virgin snow now, on a steeper incline. Her breath was thrust to the back of her throat but then surged forward in a squeal of fear as a small copse of silver birch saplings appeared to be coming straight for them.

'Hold on!' James shouted and lurched the sledge to the left of the copse.

Too far to the left. Fern felt the sledge shudder away from under them and then she was rolling, laughing and spluttering as snow filled her mouth, her ears, her hair.

She lay face down in the snow, momentarily stunned, and then her lips parted with shock as she was rolled over on to her back, her long, curly dark hair splaying out all around her in the snow.

'James, no...' Too late. His mouth covered hers, hotly and swiftly. There was a searing sensation of hot and cold and Fern struggled against him, trying to get out from under him, striving for breath.

'It's all right...' His breath was warm on her cheek. 'We're out of sight.'

'That's still no excuse——'

Once more his lips swept the protests from her own, the kiss deepening till there was no going back. His body was crushing hers under him and she felt the full power of his need. Somehow the studs of her jacket had ripped open, exposing her thick woolly sweater, but it was as if she were totally naked under his pressure. She felt her desire thrust against the clothing and she dragged her lips from his to gasp with shock.

His hand gripped her chin firmly to stop her twisting away, and then she stared up at him for the first time. His dark eyes were searching her face as if looking for the desire he couldn't hide in his own eyes. Fern bit her lip at that look, half afraid, half excited that his need was so obvious.

Slowly he lowered his mouth to hers once again, and this time she didn't struggle. Her lips were quivering with her need, and as his lips parted hers she couldn't stop the whole of her body arching willingly against him. He let out an impassioned groan as he released her chin to slide his hand under her, to add further claim to a body that was already showing that she wouldn't struggle any more.

The length of his body was urgent against hers, the soft rustle of his oiled jacket a minor disturbance in the silence that enfolded them. Fern lost herself in his kisses, which were growing more heated. She was in a different world, a white, silent world that held no memories, no past, no thoughts for what might be in the future.

His warm hand slid under her sweater, and there was breathtaking pleasure as it smoothed over her breast, ranging sensuously over her hardened nipple till she moaned in ecstasy. He lowered his head, pushing the sweater aside to gain oral access to the soft, silky curve of her skin, to draw hungrily on the engorged peak.

He moved urgently against her as his mouth came back to her swollen lips, pressing hard against her groin, so that she felt the power of his need. It excited her so deeply that her body shuddered with longing. She ached deep inside, driven by a need she had almost forgotten she possessed—a need to be held and loved and kissed and made love to. It had been so long. Once she had thought there would never be another, but now... but now she still didn't know. At this very moment, knowing that because they were lying sprawled in icy snow their need was impossible to consummate, she wondered if she would feel any different if the situation were different. Tucked up in a romantic four-poster in a remote hotel room somewhere miles away from two children and a dog and cosy domesticity? Because of that thought her body spasmed and she tensed stiffly against him.

'Don't, Fern,' he breathed against her throat.

'Don't what? Don't fight it?' Suddenly she had the strength to do just that. She shoved him away from her and struggled to her feet, pulling her sweater down and drawing her jacket hard around her. Feverishly she brushed at her sopping cord jeans, shivering now with the cold. 'How bloody predictable! What a damned... wretched... unoriginal comment to make!'

James was on his feet now and reaching out to grab at her shoulders. Fern staggered back, slipped, and he caught at her before she lost her footing on the snow.

'Listen to me and listen hard, Fern,' he growled, holding her firmly by the shoulders. 'I know and understand what is going through your mind——'

'You don't!' Fern insisted. 'You think I want you and you leave no doubt in my mind that you want me, but——'

'But that isn't enough for you, is it?' he challenged. 'Don't tell me you are a typical female when it comes down to it. You want the love commitment along with your desire——'

'Love?' she exploded, her eyes wide with shock. 'Don't be absurd! Love doesn't come into this. A relationship of whatever kind doesn't come into this. This is much more subtle, something a man would never understand.'

'Try me,' he grated, almost shaking her now.

'Why? Why should I open up to you?' she blazed, not sure if she could explain it even if she wanted to. She had only just realised it herself. It was his telling her they were out of sight of the children that had done it.

'Because, whether you like it or not, something is happening here.'

'Sure.' She shrugged dismissively. 'I'm not naïve enough not to have noticed you fancy me; you even admitted it. And, as you said, I'm open and honest—and I am. So I admit I'm attracted to you. So what happens now? We go back to the cottage and our children are waiting for us. Your daughter, my son. Your past, my past——'

'You still love your husband...'

'Yes...yes, I still love him,' Fern told him truthfully but a little shakily. 'But it isn't the issue here. I don't *live* in the past. I have wonderful memories, but they are just that—memories.' Suddenly she let her tense

shoulders sag and she widened her eyes appealingly.
'It...it goes much deeper than that. I...I...just don't
think I can do it, you know...have an affair.' She shook
her head. 'Not because of Ralph...'

'Because of Charley?' James murmured quietly.

Fern lowered her lashes and stared down at the dis-
turbed flurry of snow at their feet. 'Partly,' she whispered and then she raised her lashes to look at him and
took a deep breath. 'I'm a mother—Charley's mother.
I love being his mother; I wouldn't have it any other
way. But I can't see myself being anyone's *lover*. I can't
imagine myself arranging baby-sitters, getting dressed
up to go out to dinner, and everything that goes with
having an affair. I...I could never make love in my own
house with my child sleeping in the next room. I couldn't
make love in someone else's house or some discreet hotel
and then have to get up and go home to Charley. It
seems...tacky... I...I just couldn't do that.'

James's grip on her shoulders softened to a caress and
his eyes looked deeply into hers. 'Fern, darling, I think
you have a big problem,' he said gravely.

'It isn't a problem to me,' she told him huskily, though
she knew it was in a way. That sort of thinking meant
she had no chance to open her heart to any man, not
yet, not for a very long time.

He raised a dark brow. 'It could be. What happens
when you do fall in love? Are you really prepared to
deny it because of your son?'

Fern snaked the tip of her tongue over her cold, dry
lips. It would have to be some love for her to be able to
overcome all that she had just told him. 'I'll...I'll have
to face that...when...if...if it ever happens,' she
croaked helplessly.

James lifted her chin and lowered his warm lips to hers and Fern closed her eyes, her heart already pacing nervously. If it did happen, how would she cope? Supposing it had already happened? Supposing she was in love at this very minute?

He drew back from her at last, and lifted his hand to smooth wet hair from her face, and his voice when he spoke was raw with sensibility. 'Come, we'd better get back before everyone gets suspicious.'

The knots in her stomach unravelled, but her heart still thrashed feverishly in her breast. She looked deep into his eyes, willing him to understand.

'It's just that sort of thinking that puts me off,' Fern muttered dejectedly.

James smiled, a warm smile that did nothing to soothe her troubled mind. 'I see your point,' he said softly. 'But perhaps we can work on it. There's no rush.'

He turned away to crunch over the snow to retrieve the sledge, and Fern watched him through narrowed eyes. So he wasn't going to give up. She wasn't sure what to make of that. She did want him, though; she knew it with a heavy contraction of her heart. Fool that she was, she had wanted him from the very start, even when she had thought he was having an affair with Rachel. Now she knew for sure that he wasn't the feeling was even worse than fighting her guilt over her initial attraction to him.

But plain old desire was a far cry from love, she told herself as she trudged after him. Desire you could douse and live with. Love was a trickier chap to deal with. When love was in possession you were in trouble. Fern didn't want any trouble.

'Oh, Sara, I didn't expect you to finish preparing tea. This was my treat,' Fern protested after shedding her boots and jacket in the porch and stepping into the kitchen to see everything laid out on the table.

'Not guilty,' Sara laughed. 'I was busy defrosting two awkward children while Tim did the chores. He'll make someone a wonderful husband one day,' she added hopefully.

'Well, you're welcome to make a play for me,' Tim stated with humour. 'Though I warn you I'm a confirmed bachelor and a workaholic to boot, but the chase could be fun, Sara, if you have the stamina...'

There was more good-humoured banter between everyone till it all suddenly turned sour for Fern. She hadn't really noticed how the conversation had swung to work, probably Tim changing the course of the conversation, because he was indeed a workaholic. Sara faded out of the business-talk and now James and Tim dominated it and somehow Brussels and a certain financial conference came up. Through a foggy tunnel of words the names of Robert Edwards and his daughter Rachel filtered through, and Tim was laughing and joking about Rachel being more suited to a quick trip down to Euro Disney rather than accompanying her father to a stiff financial seminar.

Fern flicked her eyes in James's direction. He was standing by the Aga and his cord jeans were gently steaming in the heat. His eyes darkened in that instant and the colour blanched from his face, and a slice of uncertainty knifed down Fern's spine.

James Causton looked guilty. That was the only word Fern could think of to describe the change in his features.

'Where are the children?' Fern asked Tim, who was filling the kettle.

'Upstairs, blasting spaceships down black holes on the computer.' He put the kettle on the hob. 'Keep an eye on that, sis. Do you mind if I show Sara your work? I've been telling her how talented you are.'

'Feel free,' Fern uttered. She hadn't taken her eyes off James, and the thoughts that were buzzing through her head weren't nice at all. Brussels had been no coincidence. He had lied to her; she knew it for sure now. The bastard had ditched Rachel for some reason, and it was a horrible thought that she might be the reason.

As soon as they were alone James spoke, coldly, with just a hint of anger.

'Why didn't you tell me?'

'What?'

'Don't play games, Fern. Why didn't you tell me Rachel was in Brussels? You must have known before just now.'

Fern stood at the other side of the table, clenching her fists to her side. She was right; he had lied about his affair with Rachel. It was still going on. He had cancelled at the last minute, and, if Sara was right, because of her. Ironically, she should be glad that he had, but he could have had the decency to let Rachel know. The poor love-struck girl was probably still waiting for him in some hotel room. It was all she deserved, but all Fern could think of was that it was a dirty trick to play on anyone. The man had no scruples.

'So you were meeting her there——'

'No, I was not!' James denied vehemently.

'So why ask?' Fern blazed.

James lowered his head. 'You wouldn't believe me if I told you.'

'No, I damned well wouldn't! I gave you the benefit of the doubt once before.'

His eyes blazed angrily. 'So you didn't believe me when I denied it?'

'Yes . . . yes, I did, but I shouldn't have done, because now I know the truth.'

'You know nothing!' James told her hotly. 'I'm denying it once again because I want this relationship—our relationship—to go a step forward. I am *not* having and never have had an affair with Rachel, so will you forget it?'

She looked at him numbly. Oh, she wanted to, yes, she wanted to believe him and to forget the whole wretched business. But she had seen them together . . . and . . . and Rachel was in Brussels. She was so badly torn that she couldn't speak. He was looking at her so earnestly and he'd denied it so hotly, almost as if it was an insult to him that she could believe such a thing of him. Eventually Fern nodded, but couldn't say the words.

'Right, that's that over with; now to the next step. I'm not going to listen to any more of your feeble excuses about children and pasts and putting your damned motherhood before anything else——'

She found her voice. 'Just a minute——'

'We haven't got just a minute, Fern,' he said threateningly. He came towards her and Fern didn't back off, because she didn't want a fight with everyone else in such proximity. He took her by the shoulders and his voice softened considerably. 'Under this very roof at this very minute you have the answer to your inhibitions,

Fern. Your loving brother Tim, and Sara. In a few minutes we are going to sit down to tea, and you, Fern McKay, are not going to say a word. You will listen to what I'm going to say and you are not going to utter one single word of protest.'

With that he lowered his mouth to hers, and this time the kiss was so powerfully dominant that she hadn't the strength to protest; nor did she want to.

CHAPTER SIX

THE cottage was unnaturally silent, warm and peaceful. It was dark and the snow was falling softly again. Fern stood by the window and watched the snowflakes buffet the window-pane and then melt into oblivion.

She drew her satin robe around her, not her towelling dressing-gown tonight. Tonight was special.

Fern drew the velvet curtains across the window and turned to look at herself in the bedroom mirror. Her make-up was flawless as she had taken time and care with it, and with her hair, too; it curled softly around her face and lay like a frothy mantle around her shoulders. Slowly she untied the belt at her waist and let the white satin fall apart to half reveal her nakedness beneath. She lifted her hands and ran them down her warm, scented body. She felt good and knew she looked it.

She was calm now, and it was a wonder after the tea-party earlier and the skirmish to get Charley's overnight bag packed. The children had screamed with excitement at James's suggestion that he stay the night up at Bourne Hall. Tim and Sara hadn't looked at all surprised when James made the suggestion, adding that he was taking Fern out to dinner. Tim had willingly offered to take Sacha off her hands for the night as well, though Fern suspected he wanted an excuse to come back the next day; he and Sara were certainly getting on very well. There was absolutely nothing Fern could protest about.

James had gone back to the Hall with Sara and the children to get ready, and Fern had the cottage to herself till James came back to collect her.

So why was she so calm when really she should be quaking with nerves or at least be wild with James for setting all this up? Cool, calm sensibility had taken over from shock and surprise at being dominated so completely. James Causton was taking her out to dinner—and that was all!

She was ready when she heard the deep rumble of a car engine coming down the lane, and ran downstairs to open the front door.

'Well, I didn't protest, as you so forcibly instructed me not to, but I should have done,' she told him as he stepped into the hall. 'We must be quite mad, going out on a night like this.'

James laughed as he brushed a flurry of snow from the shoulder of his dark navy suit. 'It would take more than a few inches of snow to keep me in tonight, but of course if you've changed your mind we could stay in——'

'No way,' Fern insisted with a laugh. 'I haven't gone to all this trouble for nothing.'

He stood back to admire her. 'You look wonderful, but then you always do.'

It had been so long since she had received a compliment. It was a lovely feeling, though it made her feel just a little nervous. She smiled and smoothed her hands down the deep purple silk dress with its matching soft leather belt clasped at her tiny waist with an ornate silver buckle. Her high heels shot her up a couple of inches, so that he didn't quite so easily tower over her.

'Where are we going?' she asked, turning to pick up her black cashmere wrap and praying she wasn't blushing.

'The Mynah House, Guildford.' He helped her drape the wrap around her shoulders.

'Great, one of my favourite places.'

'You've been before?' he asked in surprise, turning her to face him.

Fern looked up at him and stemmed a small thread of resentment before it knotted her up. 'James,' she breathed, 'I have been out these last three years, you know. I don't want you thinking that you are freeing me from some sort of domestic drudgery for the night. I'm not Cinderella . . .'

'So there have been men in your life before,' he presumed with a smile, letting his hands drop to his sides.

She stiffened slightly at that. 'Yes, one—my brother. Sometimes we dined with his clients; sometimes we dined alone. So how about you?' she said tightly. 'Have there been women in *your* life these last years?'

His eyes narrowed and darkened 'I don't see——'

'No, you don't, do you? Different rules for the sexes.' Fern felt the evening slipping away from her. 'And I don't really want to know whether there have been women or not, because it doesn't matter——'

'But Rachel mattered.'

'Yes, she mattered, because what I thought about you and her coincided with your first dinner suggestion and the fact that you openly admitted you fancied me,' she told him sharply.

He was still smiling and lifted his hands to adjust the wrap at her throat. 'So it was jealousy.' His forefinger came over her lips as she parted them to protest. 'Joke,' he warned with a glitter in his eyes. 'Your sense of humour is pretty thin tonight.'

Fern relaxed, realising that since he had arrived she had tensed up considerably. And she had taken everything he had said so far the wrong way. She was beginning to sound as if she had an enormous chip on her shoulder.

As they slowly drove up the lane to the main road, James keeping the BMW to the tracks he had made coming down, Fern apologised.

'I'm sorry I was a bitch back there. I do seem to have lost a bit of self-confidence over the years—and my humour, I suppose. Thanks for insisting on taking me out tonight. I've been really looking forward to it.'

'You were nervous when I arrived, weren't you?'

James turned into the main road, which was free of powdery snow because of the almost constant flow of traffic turning it to wet slush.

'Yes and no. I wanted to go out to dinner with you, but...well...I don't want you to get the wrong idea.'

'You think I might expect to make love to you afterwards?'

Fern saw the twitch of humour at the corners of his lips and she really didn't find it amusing.

'Is...is it what you expect?' she asked hesitantly.

'It's what a lot of women expect these days, and before you leap at my throat screaming, "Chauvinist"——'

'I wouldn't dream of casting such aspersions,' Fern interrupted rather primly. 'You must swim in some pretty slushy circles if those are the sort of women you socialise with. I...I suppose...Rachel...'

He laughed. 'Yes, exactly—Rachel. One of this new breed of women who think they have the power to call the tune in their relationships with men.'

'Oh,' Fern murmured, not quite knowing what to add to that, so going for silence to be safe.

'Don't you want to know more?'

Fern shifted a little uncomfortably in her seat and eased the seatbelt away from her chest, which suddenly felt very tight. 'This . . . this was the point of the evening, I suppose,' she resigned, recalling how angry he had been when she had accused him of having an affair with the woman. Now he wanted to clear his conscience.

'No, the point of the evening is for us to have some time together and enjoy ourselves, and we can only do that if the air is clear between us. Rachel is fouling it up.'

Fern insisted, 'I'm *not* jealous.'

'OK, you're not jealous.'

'OK, so we've established that,' Fern told him brittly.

They lapsed into silence till Fern fidgeted again. 'Well, go on, aren't you going to tell me what it's all about? I . . . I won't say anything . . .'

'You won't have to,' he laughed. 'There is nothing to say. We've known each other some time, through her father. Robert and I have done business together in the past and we have some mutual banking acquaintances. I wouldn't say we were old friends, as Rachel stated——'

'Get to the point,' Fern interrupted good-humouredly.

'You can't wait to hear the gory details, can you?'

'Gory, are they?' Her eyes were sparkling with mischief.

'They're not even interesting,' he told her with a smile, taking a sidelong glance at her. 'Sexual harassment,' he added.

'Sexual harassment?' Fern exclaimed. 'You were sexually harassing her?'

'No, idiot, she was the one doing the harassing.'

Fern was stunned for a second and then burst out laughing.

James grinned at her. 'It's not funny—it's highly embarrassing I can tell you.'

'You're not winding me up?' Fern giggled.

'Absolutely not.'

'But...' Suddenly Fern grew serious. 'No, it's not funny. Poor Rachel. Poor you. But... but you couldn't have been very firm. I mean, you took her out, to the wine bar...'

'No, nowhere.'

'I saw you!' Fern insisted.

'I was dining alone in the wine bar when Rachel suddenly appeared. I could hardly tell her to find somewhere else to sit. Then, driving home from London one afternoon, she appeared behind me, flashing her lights in my mirror——'

'The lay-by?'

He nodded. 'I pulled up; what else could I do?'

'You didn't have to kiss her!' Fern retorted, painfully remembering that heated embrace she had witnessed as she had swept past the lay-by.

'I didn't——'

'You did!' Fern insisted even more strongly than before. 'I saw you. The exact moment I passed you were in each other's arms, lips mashed together, her arms tight around your neck——'

'Now if you had slowed down you would have seen what happened next—me, unmashing my lips from hers, unwinding her arms from my neck, and gently but firmly pushing her away from me. I wasn't kissing her, she was kissing me, and very much against my will, I can tell you.'

Fern felt her mouth curling at the corners, trying to control a splutter of laughter at his indignant pomposity.

'Then I got angry,' he went on, 'and told her to find someone her own age as I had no intentions of having an affair with her.'

'Quite a hero, aren't you?' she murmured in fun. He smiled. 'But why? I mean, why didn't you have an affair with her? She's very beautiful.'

'Come on, Fern, give me some credit for a bit of sense. A pretty face doesn't turn me on.'

'Oh,' Fern murmured.

James laughed. 'Except yours, of course, for the simple reason that you are beautiful all the way through, not just on the surface.'

'You don't know that,' she murmured, trying not to feel overwhelmed by that whopping compliment.

'But I do, you see, and besides, there's a question of chemistry. I feel it for you and not for Rachel.'

Fern felt hot all over. 'But you don't know if I feel it for you,' she insisted.

'Yes, you do; you've already admitted it, so don't try and wriggle out of it. We wouldn't be here now if there weren't that chemistry between us——'

'This is a dinner date, not a laboratory experiment,' she interjected ruefully as they pulled up in front of the canopied porch of the restaurant.

James was still laughing as they entered the warm, inviting restaurant, and Fern made a determined effort not to take him quite so seriously. This chemistry business was a bit of a worry, though. Experiments could go wrong; the whole night could go wrong; *she* could go wrong!

And that was a distinct possibility, she mused as they ordered their meal from the extensive menu, Fern choosing her particular favourites—prawns basted in lime sauce and the roasted duck marinated in crushed cherries and kirsch. The heady ambience of the restaurant and the heady ambience of James Causton was getting to her, and she was relaxing far too easily.

He was funny and kind and drawing looks of determined interest from women diners in the elegant dining-room, and Fern was proud to be out with him. And there was more. She didn't want it to be the first and the last time. She wanted just a little more of him, probably a lot more of him if she allowed her senses the freedom they hadn't seen for so long.

As they sipped their wine between courses she wondered what it would be like to make love with him, to feel his warm naked skin against hers, to have his sensual hands move over her body in lazy...no, not lazy...urgent exploration. She wouldn't be shy with him, she was certain of that. Her hands would explore, eagerly; she would match his ardour because she had that sort of warmth and giving in her heart. He would smother her body with kisses, run his tongue provocatively over her breasts, and she would touch him, yes, run her fingers down over his hard stomach...

'I hope the children have settled down for the night. Victoria can be... What are you laughing at now, Fern?' he asked in good-humoured resignation.

Fern shook her head, unable to speak for laughter. She smothered her napkin over her mouth and bit back the mirth.

'You're unbelievable, James Causton,' she breathed at last. 'What was it you said to me—you wanted me out of my cosy domesticity?—and now *you* come out with a classic like that.'

He looked slightly mollified and then smiled and reached for her hand across the table. 'I read minds,' he told her softly, and Fern nearly laughed out loud again. 'I knew what you were thinking.'

'Well, I don't think you're ready for your degree in mind-reading yet,' she told him. 'But keep on trying; you might reach GCSE level some time this century.'

He had no chance to question that as the waiter arrived with their second course. Fern watched him as he sliced into his steak and knew that her heart was slipping dangerously close to the edge. She wondered what would happen if she let it go. Would she get hurt? Not yet; she didn't want to consider that yet.

'James, can I be very personal?'

'How personal?'

'Your wife.'

'I told you—no wife.'

Fern noticed a slight tightening of his grip on his fork and wondered if she ought to let it go and not pursue what she ached to know. His wife wasn't dead, and they weren't divorced, so they must be separated, but James seemed loath to talk about it.

Fern was curious, but was she curious enough to spoil the evening? And it might. James turned to get the attention of the waiter, who was at the table immediately, and ordered some mineral water and asked if she wanted more wine. Fern said not and she knew the moment was gone.

But was his evasive action intentional? Fern thought not, but she didn't want to push it. She supposed it was something very private and possibly hurtful for him, and with a small, inward sigh of regret she pushed the thought out of her mind.

'Yes, coffee, please,' she said later and declined a liqueur with it. It always gave her a headache.

'The meal was wonderful, James,' she sighed, crumbling her napkin in her lap.

'And the company was wonderful,' he told her. 'I'd like to do this again.'

'So would I,' she told him honestly. 'It makes me feel...well...sort of my own person once again. Not just a mother.'

'I told you you shouldn't live your life just for Charley.'

'Yes, you did, didn't you?'

'Shall we take it a step further?'

Fern tensed, or was it excited anticipation straining every muscle in her body? Was she really ready for this?

She stared down at her coffee, willing it to give her some sort of answer. He had so skilfully plotted this evening for her—and himself, of course—but could she let it happen this way, almost clinically? Charley out of the way, even Sacha, this wonderful meal, and then back to her cottage to... The romance in her balked at the thought. It was all so predictable: a candlelit dinner for two... Some women would think that the only way. Oh, dear, she was certainly way out of touch, too long a mother and a widow. She conjured up a picture of her and James, passionate in the snow, almost out of control, letting their lust override their discomfort. But that was what desire was all about—making love on the spur of the moment—not like this, lacking in spontaneity.

'What have you in mind?' she eventually asked in a soft voice, her stomach knotting in anticipation, not lifting her eyes from her coffee to look at him. She had come so far, but she wasn't sure it was far enough.

'Half-term.'

She blinked her eyes up to meet his. 'Half-term?' she squeaked in astonishment.

'I don't know if you have anything planned for Charley, but Sara is taking Victoria down to Cornwall to see her grandparents——'

'Sara's grandparents?'

'No, Victoria's grandparents.'

'Your parents?'

'Er—no, maternal grandparents.' He reached for the coffee-pot.

'Your in-laws?' So he was on good terms with his wife's parents. That was something, she supposed.

'I thought Charley would like to join them.' He topped up her coffee and his own. 'They have a small hotel at Helford and most holidays Victoria goes down. I thought that as they were getting on so well together it would be company for her.'

Fern didn't answer for a while. It would be lovely for Charley to have a break, but surely the grandparents would think it a bit odd, and supposing Victoria's mother was down there...

But surely James wouldn't suggest such a thing if there were problems in his separation?

'I don't know,' Fern murmured hesitantly, stirring her coffee with deliberation. Charley had never been away from her before and... She trusted Sara and Charley was certainly very fond of her, but she remembered something Victoria had said—that she didn't have a mummy. If James wasn't a widower, then that was an odd thing to say. A denial like that from the child could have been spoken with spite. Mummy wasn't around, so therefore she didn't exist. But the grandparents did and apparently James was on good terms with them, so perhaps it was all right.

'Think about it,' James said, and Fern was grateful that he wasn't pushing her.

'Oh, I will.' Suddenly she looked alarmed. 'You haven't said anything to Victoria about this, have you? I mean, if she mentions it to Charley, then... then it could be a bit awkward if...'

'If you said no?' He frowned, as if anticipating that she would and it mattered if she did. She wondered if there was an ulterior motive taking seed somewhere in his devious mind.

She smiled. 'It's a big decision to make and impossible if Victoria and Charley are determined it's a good idea.'

He nodded. 'I understand. They can be a bit wilful. I haven't mentioned it to anyone, not even Sara, though I'm sure she wouldn't mind driving the two of them down. She's often said that Victoria can be difficult on the long drive. With Charley for company it should lessen Sara's load.'

Fern felt a ripple of disappointment. So the whole idea was to lessen Sara's load, was it? For a mad moment she had thrilled at the thought he might want her to himself while the children were away.

'If you agree, we could go down ourselves mid-week for a few days. I could do with a breath of sea air.'

Fern leaned back in her seat, relaxed, and gave him a small smile. She couldn't fight this, she just couldn't. The thought was quite wonderful, in fact her pulses were thrumming at the thought of spending so much time with him. And she did want to spend time with him, more than she ever thought possible. She stared at her near-empty wine glass. *In vino veritas*, in wine is truth.

'Helford isn't exactly on the coast, more the river,' she told him softly.

He studied her for a few seconds and then smiled. 'Don't split hairs, Fern. Sea air, river air, what does it matter?' His forefinger smoothed over the back of her hand resting on the table. Such a small, delicate touch, and yet it seared her skin with heated pleasure.

'Half-term is next week,' she told him. 'That doesn't give me much time to think about it.'

'Spontaneity has a lot to be said for it,' he uttered suggestively.

His mind-reading was improving. 'I'll think about it,' she told him with a smile.

'What about Charley's grandparents? Are they local?'

It was with her again—that feeling that they had little in common but their children. But what else could they talk about when they were so important in their lives? It occurred to her that it must be quite difficult for him bringing up Victoria single-handed. Of course, he had help, but it wasn't like a normal family unit.

'Ralph was adopted but it didn't work out very well for him, so no grandparents on his side. My own parents live in New Zealand and come over every summer to see us. They wanted me to go out to join them after...after Ralph died.' She shrugged. 'But I didn't want that. They would have smothered me and Charley.'

'I'm glad you didn't go,' James said quietly and their eyes met, and in that moment Fern was glad too.

They finished their coffee in silence, Fern lost in thought about what to do about half-term, James also lost in thought, though Fern hadn't a clue what might be going through his mind. She wished she did, so she could mentally prepare herself for whatever he was thinking—that was if it concerned her, which it probably didn't.

Sometimes she was certain that he cared for her; other times she wondered if she was just someone different in his life, someone easy to get on with because she had a child too. Or perhaps he simply had needs, but that wasn't a very bright thought. James Causton could satisfy his needs with anyone he liked. But he hadn't with Rachel and she was desirable enough, and by the sounds of it more than willing. No, this was something to do with his wife and possibly a messy divorce coming up. There was something else, though; he could still be in love with her. So was she, Fern McKay, just a filler while he waited till she came back to him?

'Are you cold?'

Fern looked up, puzzled.

'You shivered.'

Had she? She supposed she had. 'No, not cold at all.'

'Shall we go?'

His eyes locked into hers and she wondered if there was a veiled question in the dark brown depth of his gaze. Shall we go... and make love?

'Yes, yes. It was a lovely meal, James. Thank you.'

He was still holding her eyes. 'Don't sound so humble, Fern. I much prefer you when you're sparky with me.'

She wasn't even annoyed by that. She *had* sounded *ever so* grateful. She smiled. 'Sorry, it was a rotten meal and you nearly bored me under the table. Is that better?'

He grinned. 'Uriah Heeps better!'

They were still laughing when they stepped outside the restaurant.

'Oh, this is lovely!' Fern cried as huge snowflakes whirled around her head. The evergreens in the beautiful entrance to the restaurant were already heaped with snow and the old Victorian lamp-posts down the driveway sparkled like stars in a flurry of snow.

'You are lovely,' James breathed heatedly as he whirled her into his arms while they waited for the car to be delivered to the front of the restaurant.

His warm, impassioned kiss spun her like the snow-flakes that whirled around them to nestle in her hair like tiny diamonds. It was the force and the depth of the kiss that swayed all her doubts away in a blizzard of desire. She was going to let go, to let her heart lead her wherever it called. And it was calling now, softly, temptingly beckoning her.

The roads were quieter now and the snow had beaten the slush and was building up on the roads. James drove cautiously but confidently. Fern sat in silence, mes-merised by the windscreen wipers swishing backwards and forwards, piling the snow into two orderly heaps each side of the windscreen. She didn't want to think about what would happen when they got back to the cottage. She had no past to draw on to lead her the way. She didn't want to remind herself of how it had been with Ralph the first time, because that wouldn't be right.

'I hate to say this, Fern, but this weather is worsening and I'm a bit concerned about the lane. I might get down it but I doubt I'll get back up it. It's quite a blizzard.'

It was quite a blizzard and Fern's insides were icy snowdrifts suddenly. The doubts hit her then. Why couldn't he just come out with it instead of trying to make feeble excuses about the weather? And where was the openness he had mentioned and admired in her? She dredged it up from the icy caverns of her soul.

'Why don't you just come out with it, James? You want to stay the night.' There was crispness in her tone, because she certainly didn't admire *him* at the moment. She didn't want it this way. And yet it was contrary of her suddenly to be against the idea when only moments ago she had been willing to let her heart rule her. Nerves, that was what it was, a sudden surfeit of them that was tipping her reasoning backwards and forwards till she didn't know what to think or how to behave.

His grip on the steering-wheel tightened, and Fern noticed. He was angry and so was she.

'That wasn't the intention——'

'Wasn't it? I think it was——'

'I'm responsible for the weather, am I?' he interrupted tightly.

'That was just good fortune on your part,' she retorted. 'If it weren't snowing you would no doubt have thought up some other excuse to spend the night with me!'

'My God,' he breathed hotly. 'What is it with you?'

'What is it with *you*?' she stormed. 'You manipulate my son out of my house for the night so you can take me out to dinner and then you arrange the weather for your own scurrilous reasons.'

'Is this what you really expected from the evening?'

'What is "this", exactly?'

'Don't fool around, Fern,' he warned darkly.

'You're the one fooling around. Why can't you just be honest about the whole thing? Say what you mean—that you had every intention of spending the night with me——'

'And would you have agreed if I had made the suggestion so openly? If I had come right out with, "I'll take you out to dinner, Fern, and then I'll take you back to your cottage to...!"'

Fern covered her ears and squeezed shut her eyes. She felt the car beneath her shudder to a slippery halt. God, now he was going to throw her out into the snow and let her make her own way home.

He reached across and snatched her trembling hands down from her ears. 'Open your eyes and look at me!' he ordered thickly.

Fern blinked them open nervously and gazed at him in the dim interior of the car.

'You didn't like that, did you? I didn't like saying it myself, but you brought the whole evening down to that level, Fern.'

She wasn't going to take that; no, she wasn't! 'No, I didn't,' she breathed defensively. 'It's what you expected——'

'Well, you were wrong!' he interrupted harshly. 'You're not ready to give yourself to any man yet, and frankly I'm not prepared to smooth your yellow-brick road, as you put it, back to civilisation. Yes, I want to bed you, but tonight isn't the night——'

'Oh, yes, how very easy to say that now when you know you've been caught out in what you thought was a cinch for the night! "The weather's bad, Fern,"' she mimicked. '"Why don't I spend the night at your place——?"'

'Did I suggest that?' he blurted hotly. 'Because if I did the devil himself was speaking through my voice, or maybe you just heard what you *wanted* to hear!'

Stunned, Fern gazed at him, with her brown eyes as huge as ripe chestnuts. 'I...I didn't want to hear... It's...it's what you *meant* anyway. The lane would be bad, and why don't we spend the night together...?'

She heard a sudden whirring in her left ear and then a gust of cold and snowflakes whirled in through the electric window that he had opened from his side of the car.

'Yes, Fern,' he said as coldly as the wind that gusted in the open window. 'Why don't we spend the night together?' He nodded his head to the window and hesitantly Fern turned her head. In dismay she looked up at the ivy-clad front of the house and then closed her eyes in shame.

'Recognise it?'

Fern nodded meekly.

'Bourne Hall. Five more seconds and you would have heard my suggestion that you stay here for the night, but you couldn't wait. Disappointed, Fern?' He didn't wait for an answer, just snow-ploughed on, making her feel smaller and smaller with every word. 'We'll spend the night together all right. In my house, under my roof,' he said scathingly, 'where our two children are sleeping peacefully, where there is no chance of us consummating this relationship. *If* we still have one when the dawn comes.' With that he furiously pushed open his door and got out of the car, and Fern had no choice but to follow suit.

CHAPTER SEVEN

'LET me explain,' Fern started immediately they were inside the house.

'I think you've said enough for the night, Fern.'

James took her wrap. He was cool and composed now. 'Would you like a night-cap?'

'Only if it allows me time to state my case,' she told him with firmness.

'I don't think there is anything more to say. You made your feelings quite clear in the car.' His voice was cold and brittle and Fern wasn't sure if she had upset him, or if he was just having second thoughts about the whole evening and this was a perfect way of getting out of it, making her seem to be the wrongdoer.

'I didn't,' Fern said. She lowered her eyes, wishing now that she had stayed silent. It was all going hopelessly wrong. 'I admit I was in the wrong just now. I . . . I didn't know how to take the evening. I . . . mean . . .'

'You're out of practice,' he suggested.

He was warming slightly, but only fractionally. She felt he could go either way—hot or cold—depending on what she said or perhaps didn't say. She opened her mouth to try and explain, because she had been in the wrong and was now quite ready to admit it.

'Congratulations,' came an excited voice from above, and Fern and James turned to look up the stairs, both looking startled at the outburst. 'You're the father of twins.' Sara beamed over the curving banister. Hugging a knee-length bathrobe around her, she came tripping down the stairs barefoot.

Fern, with her mouth gaping open, stared wildly at her. The thoughts that flashed round her mind weren't very pleasant.

James grinned in relief. 'Griselda?'

Sara nodded and laughed. 'Mother and babes doing fine, and I think you'd better explain to Fern before she gets the idea you have a mistress tucked away somewhere.' Her eyes were sparkling mischievously, and because of that Fern let the panic drain out of her. If his wife or a mistress had just given birth not even Sara would be so indiscreet.

'Griselda is a ewe, one of Victoria's favourites,' James told her with a smile, as if he had guessed what had gone through her mind. He gave his attention to Sara, loosening his tie. 'The children . . . ?'

'Sound asleep,' Sara told him. 'The lambs came just after you left, but I didn't let on to Victoria or I'd never have got the pair of them down for the night. Matthew's with the ewes. He said they'll all start now. He's camping out in the barn.'

'I'd better get out there. Sara, could you settle Fern for the night? She's staying. Night clothes, et cetera.' He was already halfway up the stairs, having discarded his tie and now pulling off his suit jacket. 'Is Annie in bed yet?'

'No, she's in the kitchen making up flasks of coffee for Matthew.'

'Good. Ask her to make Fern a drink before she turns in.' He disappeared from the wide-galleried landing above them, and Fern blinked after him.

She had never felt so discarded in her whole life. It was hardly the end to the evening she had anticipated. She didn't want to be here, but it seemed she had no choice. She could hardly walk back to the cottage in a blizzard in high heels.

'I don't want a drink,' she murmured to Sara.

'You look as if you could use a brandy, though,' Sara suggested sympathetically.

Fern shook her head, biting her lip as she did it. That wasn't the answer. She didn't want anything to cloud her thinking from now on, and she had some to do. She was out of place in James Causton's life, never more so than now.

'Come on,' said Sara. 'Let's go up. Hardly the most romantic of finales to end the day.' She laughed softly in a vain attempt to cheer Fern up.

Wearily Fern followed her up the stairs, wondering what she looked like for Sara to sound so considerate. Probably very disappointed. She was, but not for the reasons Sara imagined. She had wanted to clear the air with James before retiring; now it seemed she wouldn't see him till the following day, and by then it might be too late. He would have had the night to consider that he had probably made a big mistake in taking her out, that she was nothing more than a naïve widow who had been so long out of the romance game that she really wasn't worth bothering with.

James passed them on the landing, pulling on a thick Aran sweater over a Viyella shirt. He had changed into dark green cords and wore thick woolly socks on his feet.

'Are you all right, Fern?'

He stopped for a second and took her by the shoulders, and Fern wondered if he would have kissed her if Sara weren't there. After her silly accusations earlier she wondered if he would kiss her again—ever!

'Fine,' she murmured, aware that Sara had discreetly carried on down the wide corridor.

'Good. Sleep well.' His lips brushed her brow and then he turned away and carried on down the stairs.

Fern let out a sigh for nothing in particular, because that kiss had been nothing in particular. She turned back along the corridor.

Sara came out of her own bedroom next to the nursery suite, carrying a flimsy nightie and a spare bathrobe.

'Will these do?'

'Fine,' Fern repeated and followed her along the corridor. At the end there was another short flight of stairs and a wide landing, and Sara opened a door.

'The bathroom is over there.' She nodded to a door across the room. 'Are you sure you wouldn't like a drink? It's no trouble.'

Fern stood transfixed in the doorway, blanching at the sight of James Causton's suit flung carelessly over the back of a Georgian bedroom chair and the huge double bed with its ornate wood-carved headboard. This was James's bedroom!

'Oh, I don't think...' Her paleness was driven away in a hot flush of colour.

Sara turned to her and suddenly went salmon-pink. Both girls were hugely embarrassed. Then Sara giggled, covering her mouth with her hands.

'Fern, I'm sorry. I just thought...well...you know.'

Fern tried to force a smile, because in any other circumstances this would be funny. But nothing was even faintly amusing after the fool she'd made of herself tonight.

'Heavens, what must you think of me?' Sara laughed, coming back out of the room and pulling shut the door, as if to remove it from view would somehow make the misunderstanding all right.

'Do all his women spend the night after the first date?' Fern asked cryptically as Sara went for a door opposite.

'You must be joking,' Sara said as she stepped into a bedroom, this one obviously not occupied. She flung the nightie and robe on to the double bed and turned to Fern. '*If* James plays, he plays away.'

'What do you mean "if"?' Fern asked with curiosity.

Sara shrugged. 'James, I suppose, has needs like any other man, but I've been with him for four years now and haven't seen much of them. He never, but never brings a woman here. That's why I thought... oh, never mind what I thought. You know, he's never made a pass at me, and I don't mean that to sound as if I've expected it, but it has happened before. My first experience as a nanny made me wonder what exactly my duties did include, if you get my drift.' She grinned. 'It's a pleasure to work for James, a man who hasn't got four pairs of hands.'

Fern sank down on to the edge of the bed, feeling all the worse for thinking James Causton was out for the main chance.

'But you expected... I mean, you thought I was staying the night with him.'

Sara looked sheepish, crossed to the window and pulled the curtains, and then turned to her.

'Did I misread the vibes?' she asked quietly.

Fern looked at her and smiled. 'Whose—mine or his?'

'Both. I know he likes you and you like him; you can't hide that, either of you.'

'And "like" is enough to go to bed together, is it?'

'Enough for some, but obviously not enough for you two.' She came and sat down next to Fern on the bed. 'I'm sorry if I upset you by putting two and two together and making three hundred, but I did get the impression that was the whole idea tonight, James suggesting Charley come here for the night and Tim taking Sacha off. Frankly I wasn't expecting James back. I thought he'd be staying the night with you down at the cottage.'

Fern shook her head and smiled ruefully. 'Frankly, that's what I thought was in his mind too. We had a lovely meal and then I got ridiculously old-fashioned, or maybe just panic-stricken about how to handle it all. I mean, I've been so long out of the games people play these days that I didn't know how to cope.' She sighed with regret. 'James started to make some excuse about the weather, implying that the car might get stuck in the snow. I thought he was about to suggest that he stay with me for the night, and I got all paranoid and female about it all. We had a few words, some not nice at all. Really, all he was going to suggest was that we stayed here tonight. He had no intention of bedding me tonight anyway.'

'Didn't he?' Sara asked with a twinkle in her eye.

Fern shook her head again. 'Now I'm absolutely sure he didn't.'

'But you wanted to?'

'No!' Fern protested, not sure if she was enjoying this girl talk. She was out of practice at that as well.

'Come off it, Fern,' Sara said with humour. 'I've seen the way you look at each other, Tim's seen it too. So what's the big deal about sleeping together? You want to, he wants to...' She shrugged her shoulders as if she couldn't see what the problem was. 'You two weren't still rowing when I called out over the banisters, were you?'

'Sort of,' Fern murmured.

Sara looked thoughtful for a few seconds. 'Are you very tired?' she asked suddenly, and Fern looked at her, startled.

'Wide awake, why?' She hoped she wasn't going to suggest a game of Happy Families to while away the night. She really wanted solitude to think.

'Right,' said Sara, jumping up. 'I'll just be a minute.' She was gone before Fern could stop her.

Fern stared down at the carpet at her feet, kicked off her shoes and curled her toes into the thick pile of the patterned Wilton, and reflected on Sara's attitude. The sleeping-together business *was* a big deal. Maybe not to Sara; she was single and free of any responsibilities. Fern had Charley and because of him she knew she couldn't be so free-thinking, and... and also in a way because of Ralph. He had been her first and only love, and somehow because of him she couldn't be... simply promiscuous.

Slowly Fern got up and moved to the window. She was fighting something here and she wasn't sure what. With a small frown she parted the curtains and looked out of the window. This side of the house overlooked the farm buildings. The snow had stopped but for a few errant snowflakes and the night sky was clear. There were lights on the sides of outbuildings, sparkling across the crisp covering of snow, and it was all brightness and light. The long barn was well lit, from the outside and inside. It had windows in the sloping roof and where the snow had slipped a golden glow broke through.

New life was coming into the world there, Fern mused, little lambs being born into a crisp, fresh white world. Suddenly Fern knew something new had come into her life, something bright and pure and so intense that it had to be acknowledged.

She knew then what she was fighting. Not James Causton himself, but he was the cause of it, this something deep within her own being. She was fighting love. Fern gathered her arms around her, because she could only draw comfort from herself. Love was in possession and she was rebelling against it, and it was causing her pain.

Should she give in? The thought was terrifying. To struggle against it would cripple her, but to give in, to go along with it, and then find that he didn't feel the same way... She mustn't think that way; it was too achingly painful. Love was a positive creature.

'Here, these should fit you,' Sara declared as she came back into the room to toss a pile of clothing down on the bed. She looked very satisfied with herself and Fern wondered what was going on in her mind.

'What's this?'

'Jeans, a couple of sweaters, socks, jacket, scarf and boots. We're about the same size.'

Fern's puzzled eyes flicked from the mound of clothes to Sara's grinning face and back to the clothes again.

'If you can't beat 'em join 'em!' Sara laughed. 'Go on,' she urged. 'Get dressed in some sensible clothes and get down there to the lambing barn.'

'What on earth for?' Fern protested.

'Because if you don't somehow clear the air between you and James before breakfast it might be too late. It will be awful if you don't, the children there as well. You'll end up not speaking, probably never again.'

'But Matthew is there and James wouldn't want me there, getting in the way!'

'You won't be getting in the way. You'll be pouring cups of coffee, mopping brows, and giving support, and it's precisely the fact that Matthew is there that means you won't row any more.'

She had a point, Fern supposed. 'I'm not sure...' she murmured.

'I am,' Sara assured her. 'If you don't you'll only lie here worrying all night. At least out there you'll be too busy to brood. I'm off to bed now, because the monsters will be up at the crack of dawn.' She turned at the door. 'Have fun.'

'Have fun,' Fern muttered ruefully to herself as she changed quickly. She couldn't have seen this happening if she had pondered for a month over the outcome of the evening.

Sara's clothes fitted her perfectly, apart from the boots, which were a bit big, but Sara had brought two pairs of socks, so she put them both on to fill out the gaps.

She slid into Sara's oiled jacket as she went down the stairs. She went through the kitchen to the back door and found Annie still in the kitchen, making a pile of sandwiches.

'Just in time.' Annie smiled. 'You can take these sandwiches down with you; Matthew will be starving.'

Fern waited while she packed the sandwiches in polythene; she stood self-consciously by the sink, wondering what James had said about her being here, because Annie didn't look at all surprised to see her.

'I beg your pardon?' Fern said weakly.

'Charley,' Annie repeated. 'He's had us all in stitches tonight. Such a mimic...'

'Yes, yes, he is,' Fern said faintly, guilt welling inside her. Annie had been talking about her son and she hadn't even been listening properly.

She was still frowning worriedly at that thought when she went outside into the crisp night air. She doubted if there had ever been a minute when Charley hadn't been in her thoughts, not till now. Now James Causton was creeping in more and more.

As she crunched through the snow towards the barn she decided she wasn't going to be negative about that; if she was, then she would indeed be leading her life solely for her son. Now she wanted more, but it didn't mean Charley would be loved less; probably more, because love seeded more love. Fern felt hot; suddenly she was so full of love that she was bubbling over with it.

Fern pushed open the huge barn door, not knowing quite what to expect. It was a huge barn, and as Fern's eyes acclimatised to the dim light and the layout stretching down the length of the barn she saw James and Matthew to the right in the pens. It was quite warm in spite of the height and breadth of the building, but that wasn't surprising, given the number of occupants.

Dozens of black-faced sheep with thick creamy coats eyed her warily as she walked down to the end of the barn. Griselda was in a pen of her own, her adorable twins feeding hungrily from her. James turned and grinned at her.

'I didn't expect you.'

Fern smiled, a bit uncertain of what to say. 'Annie made you some sandwiches. Where's Matthew?' He'd disappeared.

James nodded to the flock of sheep and suddenly Matthew's head appeared between them as he struggled to pen another sheep away from the others.

'Looks as if you've just arrived in time,' James said, leaping over the sturdy fence to give him a hand. 'Have you seen a ewe giving birth?' he asked, turning to look at her, and then laughing at the sudden paleness of her face.

'No,' she uttered weakly, 'but it looks as if I'm going to.' She slumped down on a bale of straw. She watched in awe, her eyes wide, her stomach contracting in sympathy. To Fern's untrained eye it seemed to be over in no time at all. It was twins again—yellow, matted, wet little heaps that lay exhausted in the straw till their mother licked life into them. It seemed like only minutes before the two of them were on their feet, their legs wobbly and staggering, falling down and struggling up again and again. The ewe nuzzled them, urging strength to those tiny beings, familiarising herself with her newborn offspring. Fern wiped the tears from her cheeks with the back of her hands.

'Are they all having twins?' she asked when James joined her later. She had watched in silence as the two men had worked, selecting and shifting more ewes into delivery pens. It was heavy work, and James's face was streaked with grime and sweat when he eventually slumped down beside her, grabbing a handful of straw to clean his hands. Quickly Fern scrabbled in the straw for the flasks and poured hot, steamy coffee for them all. Matthew trudged over and took his gratefully.

'Hopefully, yes.'

'And do you have names for all of them?'

Matthew laughed. 'That's Victoria. She names all her favourites.'

James made the introductions and Fern opened the sandwiches for him. Matthew took one. 'I'll bed down here for the night, Mr Causton. Those won't be the last tonight.'

'Do you foresee any problems?' James asked.

Matthew shook his fair head. He wasn't very old, maybe about twenty or twenty-one. Fern suddenly recognised him as the young man who had delivered her car back to the cottage after the night Tim had forgotten to collect Charley from school. 'I'll call the vet if there are, but I reckon not. I can handle a breech on my own if you want to turn in.'

James stood up and stretched. 'Call me if you need me, Matthew.' Slipping his arm around Fern's shoulders, he led her through the barn, Fern turning to call out a goodnight to Matthew, who waved in return.

'I thought you'd be out here all night,' she told him as they stepped out into the freezing night air.

James looked at his watch. 'We have been, almost. Do you know it's gone three?'

'Don't be silly...' She grabbed at his wrist to check for herself. 'Heavens, where has the time gone?'

'It flies when you're enjoying yourself.' He held her close to him as they crunched back to the house.

Fern laughed and supposed that was some sort of enjoyment for him. Such a contrast to his other life.

'Why a hobby farm?' Fern asked. 'Not the sort of hobby most bankers would take to.'

'You'd be surprised. I know at least five others. It's the contrast, I suppose, back to nature and all that. I come from farming stock anyway, and Victoria's fa...Victoria loves the animals.'

Fern frowned at that slight hiccup. He'd changed his mind about something he was going to say, but Fern couldn't think what it might be. She looked up at him and he smiled down at her, and she saw that he was quite exhausted.

'What made you come down?' he asked, pushing open the back door.

'Sara,' Fern told him honestly. 'She sensed an atmosphere between us and said it would be worse if we slept on it.' She turned to face him. 'She was right. We haven't talked—you've been too busy—but...but it's all right, isn't it?'

He slid his arms around her waist. 'Yes, I've forgiven you and now I want to put it behind us——'

'But I haven't explained.'

James slid Sara's jacket from her shoulders and hung it up on the back of the door. He took off his own and hung it over hers. 'You don't have to,' he said quietly, 'because I do understand.'

'How can you?' Fern breathed, wanting desperately to talk about it. But perhaps now wasn't the time. He was tired.

He gathered her into his arms. 'I've pushed you, Fern. You're not ready yet...'

'So you keep telling me, but...but I am...ready, I mean.'

He looked at her doubtfully, his dark eyes flicking across hers. 'Are you saying you want it to be tonight?'

'W-why not?' she murmured, wondering at her own nerve.

'To get it over with as if it's some sort of penance?' He shook his head and released her. 'Not that way, Fern.'

Suddenly she was angry, with him and herself. He was making her sound as if she were begging for it. That was bad enough, but the worst feeling of all was that she was beginning to think he didn't want her any more.

'So what way?' she blurted. 'And...and when? I mean...when am I supposed to know?'

His eyes darkened. 'What the hell are we talking about here? Sex? Just sex?'

'N-no...'

'What, then?'

Fern stepped back, wishing herself away from here. 'I...I don't know——'

'You don't know much, do you?'

'Damn you, James Causton!' she thrust back at him. 'You confuse me——'

'You confuse yourself, Fern——'

'Because I don't know how to take you! Because I don't know what or how you feel!'

'Does this help?' He wrenched her into his arms and his lips were on hers instantly, in a kiss so powerful that it jerked alive every sense in her confused body. Suddenly she was pressed back against the door, the whole length of his body hard against hers. Her lips parted with shock rather than desire, her body stiffened and fought his, and then a betraying force took over and she shuddered against him.

She thought the kiss was a punishment, the pressure down her body a cruel whiplash for her persistence. And she had been persistent, she realised, forcing him into something he wasn't ready for, but she had thought she was.

But she was ready, her heart told her. She wasn't going to fight it; she had promised herself that. Love fought was a struggle; love yielded to was easier to live with... though only if it was returned.

His kisses grazed from her mouth to her throat and his arms around her moved to press her body hard into his, where she felt every need bunched against her. He wanted her; of that she had no doubt. He cared for her; of that she had no doubt. But love?

His hand moved from her back to the front of Sara's sweater, ran over her breasts, and then smoothed down to the top of her jeans, then further down between her thighs. His lips came back to hers, swollen with passion and need as he cupped her.

Fern locked her arms around his neck, her thumbs pressing into his flesh. Her heart beat wildly, and her love and her need urged her on, but suddenly she was useless, hesitant and not knowing what to do. She wanted to be led, for James to make every move, for him to tell her what to do...

There was indecision then, a fear that she would make a fool of herself. She wanted it to be perfect and was terrified that it wouldn't be...

'What's wrong?' James breathed heavily, nuzzling his lips across her chin. 'I thought this was what you wanted.'

Fern's body stiffened even more. 'But I doubt it's what you want,' she told him sourly and pulled out of his arms. 'Don't be so patronising, James. I'd like you to make love to me because you're driven by passion and need, not because you think I need teaching a lesson.'

James shook his head in disbelief and raked a hand through his hair. 'I can't win.'

'No, you can't, and it seems nor can I,' she stated despondently as she swept out of the kitchen and headed back up to her room.

She threw off Sara's clothes and tossed them on the bed, then relented and folded them neatly and put them on a chair. She needed the bathroom and was pleased to find she had an *en suite*. She showered away the grime of the barn, though she could do nothing to rid herself of her need for James to love her. What a mess she'd made of the whole evening and half the night.

She snuggled down into the bed and knew she wouldn't sleep. The bedside lamp threw shadows across the room and she studied them, trying to get her thoughts and feelings into order, but it was far too difficult a task to deal with. At last she reached for the lamp and switched it off, and, as the darkness softened around her, suddenly she was very tired.

The soft pressure on her lips drew her up from a hazy warmth. The smooth caresses down her naked body aroused her sleepy senses. She moved hungrily against his body, felt his nakedness bearing down on her, soft and heated and yet tense and hard.

It was a beautiful dream and yet not a dream, and Fern hovered somewhere on the brink of consciousness. The feeling was delicious, and she spread her arms around his back and wanted far more than this delicious feeling. She ached deep inside, felt a burning sensation rising up from her groin.

She moaned softly and the pressure eased slightly away from her, and then as his mouth moved to her breast she was awake and yet still floating in a dream-like state.

She parted her lips in the darkness as he drew tenderly on her breast, running his tongue tantalisingly around her swollen nipple, arousing her desire till she moaned softly again.

There was no panic now, no indecision. James had made the choice for her and now she knew she would never have been able to make it for herself.

She was confident now too, not afraid to show the man she loved that she wanted him, because he had come to her because he had needed her. Her hands moved as eagerly as his and this time as her mouth brushed feverish kisses across his jawline he moaned softly too. Almost a release for him, as if he too had been unsure.

There was no need for words. Their heated breath and the movement of their exploration of each other was enough. Fern splayed her fingers across his chest as he raised himself up to look down on her in the eerie half-light of a new day, maybe wanting to reassure himself that she was indeed awake and aware of what she was doing. She half smiled up at him and then he came down to her lips once again, sliding his arms firmly around her and clasping her tight to him.

Fern clung to him, the ache deepening to a definite pain, the longing for him so total that there was nothing more she wanted from life. His touch became more urgent; the desperate urgency she had so longed for was there to feel, to breathe, to absorb. She felt passion, something she had known nothing about these last years, something she had thought she would never experience again.

She touched him as he parted her thighs, and smoothed her hand around him, fingers only slightly trembling against his taut silken flesh. He groaned at that touch, a deep, throaty sound torn from him as if she had power over his life and he couldn't fight it.

He thrust into her at last and Fern arched up against him, parting her lips in a silent, delicious, exquisite agony of need. His power was so intense that Fern felt the swell of her ecstasy, so very near to the edge of sweet oblivion. The fire inside her threatened to engulf the life from her limbs. She struggled to hold on, to hold back from him, to delay the burst of liquid fire within her, and then it was too late and she cried out, and James's mouth closed over hers to stem her cry of freedom. That kiss was all he needed to let go himself. They were suspended for one brief ecstatic second of searing heat, and then the pulsing, throbbing thrust of their climax dispersed in a vortex of molten pleasure, flowing, flowing, like liquid gold.

Sleep was almost instantaneous; like a drug, it enveloped them. There was no room for talk or thoughts, just a heavy languidness as they lay exhausted in each other's arms.

Fern was woken by the savage rays of light that blurred around the edge of the curtains. Sun was demanding admittance, almost indecently. Fern stretched and reached out for James, and, as inevitable as the new day, he wasn't there.

She hadn't really expected him to be, and she understood. She strained her ears for sounds of life, for sounds of children.

The door slowly opened and Fern turned her head, half expecting her son's face to appear around the edge of the door.

'Breakfast in bed,' James told her, kicking shut the door with his foot. He put the tray down on the dressing-table and then went back to the door and locked it.

'Where...where are the children?' It was a question that had no place after last night—or rather this morning—but it was inevitable. A sudden depression hit her. Not regret—she couldn't regret what had happened; it was just a sudden feeling that life went on and where was it going?

James, in a dark blue towelling robe, poured coffee and then brought the tray to the bedside table.

'Dressed and out of our lives for a couple of hours.'

'The lambs?' Fern murmured as James discarded his robe and, naked, slid into bed next to her. Funny, but that was the first glimpse she'd had of his wonderful body. And it was quite magnificent, broad and powerful, skin golden, just enough dark hair across his chest and down over his flat stomach.

'Where else? It will keep them fully occupied for quite a while, long enough for us to have a leisurely breakfast and then make love again.' He thrust a slice of buttered toast in her mouth before she had a chance to protest.

Fern plumped up the pillows, her mouth full of toast, and then slumped back against them, leaning her head against the pine headboard.

'James——'

'Don't speak with your mouth full; it's bad manners.'

He lay back with her, his coffee-cup perched on his chest. Fern swallowed. 'I thought I was dreaming...'

'You thought nothing of the sort,' he teased.

She smiled and reached for her coffee. 'You made it easier for me.'

'And I made it easier for myself, Fern. I couldn't bear the thought of you sleeping under the same roof and not possessing you.' He put his cup down on the tray, leaning over her to do it. He lowered his lips to hers and then drew back to murmur, 'Don't kid yourself I was doing you all the favours.'

She laughed, because she knew that not to be true. He could make out he was chauvinist of the century, but Fern knew better. It had been the only way, and they both knew it. Last night she had been crippled with self-doubt, not able to cope with the whole situation. Remarkable for a woman who had been married for two years and was the mother of a six-year-old. But it was probably because of that that she had felt so terribly insecure about having a relationship with a man again.

She had coped with Ralph's death, bringing up Charley on her own, and had almost resigned herself to a celibate life till Charley grew up. Then she had fallen in love, and the shock of that had swept away the past and she had been a novice lover once again, not knowing how to behave, not knowing how to flirt or show her true feelings. Motherhood had taken away her confidence and individuality.

'James——'

'No, Fern!' James breathed firmly but softly at her throat. 'This is our time and I need you.' As he drew down the sheet she was clutching to her chin, to expose her warm naked body, he showed his need.

Willingly she gave her body; not so willingly she held back a small part of her heart. Yes, James had a need, and she too, and as his kisses and caresses proved it she knew that there had to be something more. The bright new day brought bright new doubts that hadn't been around when James Causton had crept into her bed before.

She didn't want to think about those doubts, because she had chosen to be positive about her love. It was in possession and she was going with it, but she wondered about James. Did he love her? If he did, would he go with it or would he fight it? Maybe for the sake of his daughter? Or...

No, she couldn't allow such thinking. She forced a protective mist around the thoughts as James moved urgently against her more than willing form. When he was in her arms and loving her like this there wasn't room for doubts or fears.

CHAPTER EIGHT

FERN knew it would have to come, the doubts overwhelming her again till she felt guilt wrapping itself around her throat to stifle her. It had been all right while they were cocooned in the bedroom, but coming out and knowing the children were around tensed Fern's nerves.

'Mummy, the lambs have come!' Charley shouted across the barn.

Victoria ran to her father and eagerly clutched at James's hand as he and Fern entered the barn, pausing to kick snow from their boots. Fern was wearing Sara's clothes again and wondered if the children would notice. She was madly self-conscious, but then suddenly thought how ridiculous her attitude was. The children were too young to understand the implication, and besides, they had more important matters on their minds—cute little woolly bundles.

'We've picked names for Griselda's lambs,' Victoria cried with excitement, pulling at James's sleeve. 'Larry and Snowy. Larry is mine and Snowy is Charley's.'

Fern and James laughed. James swung his daughter up into his arms and they joined Charley at Griselda's pen.

'Can I take mine home?' Charley pleaded, hanging over the fence, swinging his legs.

'Don't be silly,' Victoria told him sharply, sliding out of James's arms and joining Charley to hang over the fence. 'You can't take lambs away from their mother.

You can come every day to see him, though, can't he, Daddy?'

'If Charley wants to,' James told his daughter.

Fern stood back from them all, her stomach knotting. She could see her son slipping easily into all their lives, but where did she stand? A very limp onlooker, by the appearance of things.

James crossed the barn to have a word with Matthew, who was heaving bales of hay for the flock to feed from, and Fern watched the two children dashing across to the next pen to gaze in wonderment at the other new-born lambs.

'Do you want to leave Charley here for the day?' Sara asked.

Fern jumped and turned to her, so deep in thought and self-pity that she hadn't seen or heard Sara come into the barn.

'Not really,' Fern told her with a sigh, 'but he's having such a good time. . . .'

'Leave him, then,' Sara suggested brightly. 'I'll bring him down later.'

Fern was hesitant. Charley was liking it too much here, and what would happen if. . . ? 'I couldn't. I mean, it's not fair on you. You have enough to cope with.'

'It's easier with two, would you believe?'

Fern smiled. 'Yes, I would believe. I often wish I'd had another, a brother or sister for Charley.'

'Victoria wouldn't be so spoiled if she'd had a sibling rival. James dotes on her and she on him. You know, we've all noticed a difference in her since Charley came into her life. She never stops talking about him. He's the brother she never had.'

Fern was flattered on behalf of Charley, but a little worried for both of them. Everyone was getting far too close for comfort. There it was again, that niggling doubt. She knew exactly how she felt about James, but his feelings for her were very uncertain.

'How…how long have James and his wife been apart?' Fern had to force the question out. She longed to know, though really she should ask James; but he always seemed so reticent about talking about his personal life. It was cheating a bit to ask Sara, but the need to know was strong enough to outweigh her guilt.

'You don't know?'

Fern wasn't sure how to take that. Sara had said it as if she expected that James would have confided in her by now.

Fern hunched herself into her jacket. 'No, I don't know.'

'You, me and the rest of the world,' Sara said, which so surprised Fern that she opened her eyes wide in astonishment. 'Except Annie, of course,' Sara went on. 'She's been with James for years and years. But I'm afraid it's a closed shop there as well. Loyalty with a capital L.'

'How do you mean?' Fern quizzed, her curiosity flaming now.

'James is a very insular person where his private life is concerned and very protective over Victoria. I just get the impression that the split was very painful, so painful it's a taboo subject and no one wants to talk about it.'

'Oh,' murmured Fern. She had suspected that for herself. Was James still in love with his wife and so hurt by the breakup that he had denied her existence? He had said, 'No wife', as if she didn't exist for him any more.

But he wasn't divorced; he had denied that and she believed him.

'But what about Victoria's grandparents down at Helford?'

'Oh, you know about them?'

'James told me you take Victoria down in the holidays.' She didn't want to mention James's suggestion that Charley accompany them next time.

'They are lovely,' Sara enthused. 'They adore Victoria, but, you know, they never mention their daughter. It makes you feel that something grim happened in everyone's past and the whole family has closed ranks against outsiders. James is very close to them, which makes you wonder if Victoria's mother ran off with the gamekeeper, leaving James holding the baby.' She laughed. 'Imagine any woman turning down James Causton for a gamekeeper. If she did she must have been bonkers!'

Fern laughed with her, but her mirth was hollow. Sara's surmise could be very close to the truth. Maybe James's hurt pride was the key to the denial of a wife.

'So it's settled. Charley stays and I bring him down later.'

Fern noted the sparkle in Sara's eyes, and the truth began to dawn. 'You wouldn't be hoping to run into my brother by any chance, would you?' she asked knowingly.

Sara grinned. 'Would you mind?'

Fern shook her head. 'I wouldn't, but you... you know——'

'He's a confirmed bachelor?' Sara giggled. 'Some men just say that to make the chase more interesting and intense. They're all little boys at heart, just aching to be mothered and smothered, and I've plenty of experience of that.' She laughed again. 'Plenty of experience with children, that is,' she emphasised. 'Victoria! Don't do that!' She ran off to rescue Charley, who seemed to have been buried alive by Victoria in a heap of straw, but at least he was laughing.

James's daughter certainly seemed to have the upper hand in the relationship with her son, Fern mused. The dominant female. Fern wished she had some of her spirit, then perhaps she could winkle out of James the mystery of his disappearing wife.

James caught Fern at the barn door. 'Where are you going?'

'I must get back,' Fern told him, forcing cheerfulness to her tone. 'I've got orders to pack up for the post this morning. Sara said Charley can stay; is that all right with you?'

'Our pleasure. I'll bring him down later.' They stood outside the barn, Fern cold now for standing around so long.

'Well, actually...' Her eyes were bright as she looked up at him. 'Not that I wouldn't love to see you, but...'

'The brush-off so soon?' His eyes were dark pools of anything but the brush-off he'd suggested.

'No,' Fern laughed. 'Not yet; you're just beginning to get interesting,' she teased.

'You always were,' he told her with a grin, and bent to run his mouth across hers.

'Pooh, you smell of sheep,' she laughed, wrinkling her nose.

'Very romantic,' he sighed, slipping his hand around her shoulder and turning her towards the house. 'So why don't you want me to bring Charley back?'

'Sara said she would. Tim is bringing Sacha back this afternoon and I have a feeling a romance is brewing.'

'Aha,' he breathed. 'And I wonder who instigated it in the first place?'

'I wonder,' Fern said innocently. 'Hey, I'm going the wrong way.' She stopped by the last barn. 'I'll cut across the fields; that's if you don't mind.'

'I'll drive you down.'

Fern raised a brow and smiled knowingly. 'Last night you were worried about not getting the car back up the lane. The snow didn't rise up and disappear in the night, you know.'

'It did first thing this morning,' he said mysteriously.

'Oh, yes?' Fern drawled and kicked her feet in the powdery snow. 'What's this, then—self-raising flour?'

He cupped her chin in his hand. 'I had one of the farm-hands take the tractor down to clear the lane for you. Not a very clever idea, I'm beginning to think.'

'No, now you have no excuse for dropping me off and coming straight back home.' She grinned.

'Don't get too smart, Fern McKay.' He dropped a kiss on her lips. 'I might just have to hang around for a while as I help you out of Sara's clothes. Poor thing; she lives in rags on the pittance I pay her. That's her best sweater and jeans, and you wouldn't want her not looking her best for your brother, would you?'

As his arms enfolded around her, drawing her hard against what was obviously his intention for the next few hours, she laughed and submitted and murmured, 'Now who's getting smart?'

Fern was glad she hadn't mentioned anything to Charley about going away with Victoria for half-term. The snow had persisted on and off and James didn't want Sara to risk the treacherous roads, so the trip was cancelled.

The lane had been kept clear by James's workers, so there was no problem getting in and out. James was a frequent visitor and Fern suspected he'd kept the lane clear for his own purpose, which was a nice thought.

Fern adjusted the pattern she was working on and with a mouthful of pins reflected that Charley's world had changed dramatically as well as her own. He had a playmate now. He and Victoria were inseparable, and though Fern should feel delighted that her son was so happy she wondered what the future would hold for them all.

Fern took the pins from her mouth and pushed aside the patterns impatiently. If the truth were admitted to she was worried sick about the whole business. Charley was up there now, at Bourne Hall. He wanted to be there all the time, with Victoria and the animals, and Annie spoiling him and fattening him up, and Sara looking after him so well that he didn't even notice when his own mother wasn't around. Even Sacha was allowed up at the Hall now. She wasn't allowed near the stock, but happily freaked out in front of the Aga in the kitchen and snapped at titbits that just happened to come her way—frequently!

'Oh, no,' Fern groaned as she peered out of the window. She'd heard the car and hoped it was James, but his visits were usually confined to the evenings. Usually, but not always. It would be sod's law if he turned up now, when the cottage was in such a mess and she was up to her armpits in orders to get out—and now Rachel was here!

Fern opened the front door to Rachel, not knowing quite what to expect, but anticipating that this was hardly a friendly call.

'Where's Charley?' Rachel asked as she went through to the kitchen, taking off her coat and turning to hand it to Fern. Fern took it and draped it carelessly over the back of the armchair by the Aga.

'Out,' Fern told her, but didn't offer more. Since when had Rachel shown an interest in her son?

Fern filled the kettle, thinking that Rachel didn't look at all bad after having been rejected by James, but it was some time back and she must be well over it by now. She wondered what she was doing here, but didn't ask. If she did she knew she wouldn't be able to mask her hostility from her, and there was hostility. She couldn't forget how Rachel had tried to put her down in front of James that night.

Fern put the kettle down far too hard on the hob, which wasn't very smart, she supposed; it showed she was annoyed and was possibly unnerved by Rachel's presence.

'So apparently Tim has a girlfriend,' Rachel said silkily.

Fern couldn't conceal her surprise at that. Whatever Rachel's reason for dropping in like this, she hadn't expected Tim to be the cause. She hoped she wasn't in pursuit of her brother again. The girl really had an insatiable appetite for men.

'Did he tell you about Sara?' Fern asked quietly, hoping her brother hadn't told Rachel about her and James as well.

'Tim doesn't talk to me about his private life, but this is a small community and they have been seen together.'

'So?' Fern murmured, trying to remember if Rachel preferred tea to coffee.

'So nothing. I don't care a toss who Tim sees. I'm more concerned about you, Fern. I can be quite frank with you, can't I?' She didn't wait for a yes or no to that. 'It won't work, you know.'

'What won't?' She tried to regulate her heartbeat, but it was hard when she didn't know exactly what Rachel was getting at.

'Don't keep playing dumb with me, Fern. I can see where you're trying to go, but I can assure you it's a dead end. If you think you can ingratiate your way into James Causton's household by fixing his nanny up with Tim you might as well know you haven't a hope in hell.'

Confident that Rachel knew nothing about her relationship with James, Fern let her heart beat normally once again.

'I introduced Tim to Sara, yes,' Fern admitted. 'And very well they're getting on too...'

'A nanny... Just about your dumb brother's mark——'

'Quite a dumb family altogether, aren't we?' Fern breathed sarcastically. She was desperate to hold her temper, but she couldn't hold back her scathing sarcasm; that was asking too much of herself.

'Yes, it does seem a family trait. That's why I'm here really. I hate to see the afflicted make fools of themselves.'

'I don't think Tim is making a fool of himself over a sweet, honest girl like Sara.' Now Fern *was* playing dumb. She had a fair idea where this was all leading, and she was certain Rachel wasn't referring to Tim but to herself, but she wasn't going to give Rachel an ounce of satisfaction.

'I hear Charley spends quite a lot of time up at the Hall. Is that part of the plan too?'

Fern shrugged and looked at Rachel innocently. 'Of course; I'll use every opportunity I can to bring Tim and Sara closer together.'

That wasn't what Rachel wanted to hear, and her eyes narrowed wickedly because she wasn't getting anywhere. 'You've never liked me, have you?'

Again Fern shrugged, a dismissive gesture that she knew would rile Rachel even more. 'I've never given it much thought to be honest, Rachel. I never was one to bother with triviality in my life, but I'll certainly give it some thought if you want me to.' Fern reached for the cups and the teapot.

'You know, you're nothing but a suburban mother with nothing to talk about but your son,' Rachel drawled on spitefully.

The classic woman scorned, Fern mused as she made the tea, only half listening. She knew what Rachel was trying to do, and could take it. This was where her past came in useful. She'd had enough pain and hurt in her life to be able to put up a barrier.

'Are you listening?'

'Yes . . . yes, of course, Rachel. "Suburban mother", you were saying.'

'Suburban mothers don't get to marry wealthy financiers, Fern,' Rachel spiked meaningfully.

Fern smiled, though she wished her stomach wouldn't tighten so nerve-rackingly. So Rachel did know something, but how much? Had they been seen at the Mynah House when James had wined and dined her? Had someone from James's household been gossiping? Had Rachel been following James again? She couldn't ask;

she really didn't want to know. She poured two mugs of tea and handed one to Rachel.

'Are you referring to me?' She let out a dreamy sigh. 'Wish that I knew one.'

'Don't come over all innocent, Fern. You have one on your very doorstep—James Causton.'

'Oh, James,' Fern said in surprise, though she wasn't at all. 'Yes, a lovely man and a kind neighbour.' She wished he were here now, to put Rachel in her place as he had done once before, because she couldn't do it...or could she? 'He's hardly eligible, though,' she murmured, sipping her scalding tea. 'He's married with a daughter.'

'Huh, no one I know has ever seen this wife!' Rachel bit back. 'And not much of the daughter either. In fact——'

'In fact until that night you were here with Tim you didn't even know he had one, did you?' Fern delivered brittly. She'd had enough of this and was going to have to tell her to go.

Rachel coloured, but only for a flash of a second, and then she was all cool composure once again. 'She never comes up in the conversation. James and I have far more intimate things to talk about when we're together.'

Present tense, no past, Fern realised instantly as the words hit her. Rachel was implying that she still had some sort of relationship going with James, and Fern knew with a certainty that she hadn't. James spent far too much time with her to have any left over for Rachel. Suddenly Fern felt sorry for her. She doubted that Rachel even cared for James. She was just a rich spoilt bitch who wanted whatever she set her eyes on. She wouldn't even like James if she had seen him helping to deliver those lambs, but that was the James Causton Fern loved.

'Oh, you are together, are you?' Fern asked pointedly, and as Rachel smiled knowingly Fern knew that she had no idea how close she and James were getting. Rachel was here to warn her off, not knowing it was far too late for that.

'I don't want you getting in the way, Fern.'

Fern widened her eyes. 'I'm flattered you think I might, but what makes you think I'm in the running for him?'

Please don't let her come up with 'lonely widow bringing up a child on her own and needing someone to lean on' syndrome; she couldn't bear that.

Rachel suddenly seemed more relaxed now, as if she realised that Fern wasn't in fact a threat. 'Oh, I suppose I jumped to too many conclusions that night Tim forgot to pick up Charley. Poor James. I cringed for him. That's not his lifestyle at all, and you pale and anguished over your son. No wonder James shot out of here like a fireball. The man was probably dying a thousand deaths. After that night Tim mentioned that Charley spends a bit of time with his daughter, and I admit I thought you might be interested in him, but now I realise that James is more interested in Charley as a playmate for his daughter than you as a playmate for himself. Do you see much of him?'

Fern nodded, seeing no reason to deny it, but her heart was like unleavened bread in her chest. 'Quite a bit.'

'He probably feels sorry for you, Fern. Lonely widow on her own——'

'More tea, Rachel?'

Rachel put her mug on the hob and straightened her silk shirt. 'No, thanks. But you get my point, don't you?'

'Not really, Rachel,' Fern breathed resignedly. 'I can see what you are trying to do—to warn me off. I understand that, but what I don't understand is why you feel so threatened by me, a humble widow and mother. You say you know James intimately, and yet you have such little confidence in yourself and your relationship with him. You get *my* point, don't you?'

Fern watched the tide of colour rise up from Rachel's throat with interest. Blushing didn't suit her or flatter her.

'I have far more to offer James than you ever could, Fern. We mix in the same circles. Daddy knows him well and in fact is about to secure me a job in James's company. So leave him alone, Fern, I don't want you interfering,' she told Fern firmly, in control once again.

'I have no wish to, Rachel,' Fern said kindly. She could afford to be magnanimous, knowing there was no relationship between them and never could be. She trusted and believed James when he denied there was anything between them.

'Good,' said Rachel, reaching for her coat. 'Just so long as you know the situation. I wouldn't like you to think you had a chance with him when it's obvious you haven't; limitations and knowing them and all that.' She smiled condescendingly at Fern.

'Yes, thank you, Rachel,' Fern said humbly, 'Thank you for putting me right. Heaven forbid that I should make a pass at the mighty Causton. Lordy, I knows my place all right.' She made a little curtsy behind Rachel's back as she slipped into her coat. Her ridicule was lost on Rachel.

'I must get on—hairdresser's in half an hour.' She turned and looked pointedly at Fern's cascading mane of chestnut hair, which hung, unruly, around her shoulders, and then buttoned her coat.

'No work today?' Fern asked at the front door, more for conversation to show she wasn't rattled by Rachel's visit than for interest, though she was deeply rattled, and annoyed with herself for letting it happen.

'It didn't work out working for my father, and Daddy thinks I'll be better placed with the Causton organisation. James is coming to dinner tonight to talk it over. Soon I'll be seeing even more of James.'

So now Fern knew what her words of warning were all about; she was just clearing the path for another attempt at winning James, and it was going to be tonight.

Rachel smiled sweetly, which Fern took as maliciously. Fern smiled back maliciously, which Rachel took as sweetly.

'I'm glad you understand, Fern. Your time will come.'

Fern felt so sick that she wanted to go to bed for a week. James couldn't be having dinner with her tonight, he just couldn't! She was determined this wasn't going to pull her down, absolutely determined!

'Rachel!' Fern called out as Rachel picked her way through the ice and snow to her car. 'Thanks for the flowers the other week; it was sweet of you!'

Rachel waved her hand like the Lady Bountiful and skidded off up the lane.

'You bitch! You bitch! You bitch!' Fern cried, hammering her small fists on the back of the front door after she had closed it, wishing she had had the guts to scream it to her face. But that would have showed Rachel she had scored. Furiously she gave the door one last thump and then slumped wearily back against it, biting her lip in a fearful and painful attempt at control. She had taken all that mishmash of Rachel's wishful thinking on James's part. Rachel had no chance with the man, but nevertheless she had succeeded in shaking Fern's confidence. It was that playmate bit that had sliced into Fern. Charley was Victoria's playmate, and was she James's? And was James spending so much time with her simply because their children had bonded so successfully? Damn you, Rachel, damn you to hell!

'I just don't want Charley to go, James. I'd planned on taking him myself in the summer. For God's sake leave me something to do for my own son!'

'It will be company for Victoria——'

Oh, God, he was missing the whole point. 'James! Are you deaf or something——?'

'And don't speak to me as if I were one of the children!' James blazed. He snatched at one of the garments she was packing up and flung it down on the table. Fern snatched it back and smoothed it out before folding it neatly and sliding it into a large Jiffybag.

'Well, stop acting like one,' she told him sulkily, 'and keep your voice down; Charley's asleep.'

'God!' James seethed, raking his hand through his hair. 'Do you know what we sound like?'

'Yes—parents! Terrifying, isn't it?'

She looked warily at James now. His anger seemed to have evaporated. He came round the edge of the table and pulled her into his arms and held her head against his shoulder. She nearly gave into the warmth of his hold, nearly succumbed to his kisses on her tousled hair. She was fighting her love now, giving herself all the agony and anguish that she had vowed she would avoid. And all because of a few words yet to be spoken, a few words that would relieve the pain of wondering where she stood in his life and his heart.

'What is it? Why are you drawing away from us all?' he whispered.

'Us all' were the two key words in that question, Fern thought ruefully, letting her head rest on his shoulder for a few seconds. Her life had been taken over by this man and his family and household, and that would be all right if James loved her and wanted her in his future, but there was no show of that. But was she being unfair? James cared; she knew that...

She drew back from him. 'I want to take Charley to the Science Museum myself,' she told him in a small voice. 'I've always promised him——'

'This isn't what all this is about,' James grated. 'There's got to be more.' She didn't answer and he tipped her chin up. 'Fern, let's get away for a few days, on our own. No children, no dog. Sara can——'

'Look after Charley too,' she finished for him.

'And what's wrong with that?'

Fern turned away from him to clear away her work. 'Nothing, I suppose,' she uttered dejectedly. 'He practically lives with you all anyway.'

'And you object to that?'

Fern sighed. She didn't know if she did or didn't. All she knew was that everything had shifted; she no longer felt she was Charley's mother any more. Just as when they had lived with Tim she had felt she was losing her son. But that wasn't everything. James was right; there was more.

She faced him. 'James, why didn't you tell me you were having dinner with Robert Edwards and Rachel the other night?'

There was such a long silence that Fern thought he was probably weighing up what to tell her, or, worse, what not to tell her. She had battled with this one over the last few days, tried desperately not to give in to jealousy. She had reasoned that it probably wasn't true, that Rachel had just been inventing the whole thing to warn her off. But she didn't know, because she hadn't seen James that night nor the next day, and when love was in possession doubt and suspicion were always unwelcome visitors.

'How did you know?' he asked at last, his voice low and almost regretful that she knew.

Fern felt a terrible dragging feeling clawing at her insides. So it was true; they had dined together and he hadn't told her, had *chosen* not to tell her, so he must feel some sort of guilt about it. She couldn't bear it. She walked determinedly out of the room and into the sitting-room to kneel down and jam another log on the fire. She sat back on her haunches and glared fiercely at the flames, which were the only light in the darkened room.

James sat on the sofa behind her and drew her up from the floor and into his arms. 'Jealousy... And I thought it was something serious,' he murmured.

'It isn't something to be mocked,' she blurted, hurting deep inside to think he would take it so lightly. She tried to pull out of his arms, but he held her firmly.

'Fern, I didn't tell you because I expected just this reaction from you. How did you know I was going to have dinner with them?' he persisted.

Fern pulled away from him and sat up to hold her head in her hands. 'She came round to warn me off, to remind me that I'm nothing but a...' She trailed off; no need to remind James Causton of what he already knew. Suddenly she couldn't say any more, because Rachel and her wickedness had no place here. She trusted James and she wasn't jealous. It was just an excuse for how she really felt—that she had no place in his life, just as Rachel had said.

'She saw you as a threat,' James urged.

Fern nodded and swallowed hard, trying to form the words in her throat. 'She...said she was going to work for you, that her father had set it up——'

'Fern, it was one of those business dinners. Robert and I had a few things to discuss and the job in my organisation for Rachel came up. I made it quite clear that I couldn't consider her for a position because she hasn't got what it takes. It was quite amicable. Robert understood, and that's all there was to the evening. Some business talk and that was all. If Rachel led you to believe it was anything else, then it shows her ignorance and spite.'

'I know, I know,' Fern murmured, and she did, and it helped, and she despised herself for her own feelings of insecurity.

His hand had crept up her back and Fern bit her lip at the tender caress. Gently he pulled her back into his arms and his mouth sought hers eagerly.

'Darling Fern, don't put problems in our path.' His lips parted hers and he started to loosen the tiny buttons at the front of her silk shirt, and Fern clung to him as he smoothed a hand across her breast.

How easily he could arouse her; how easily he could smooth the path to lovemaking. He gave so much and yet he didn't give what she wanted more than anything else in the world—those few words of love that would make it all right and banish her insecurity once and for all. She had never felt insecure with Ralph, and, though she hated herself for the comparison, it was none the less there in her heart. Her love for Ralph had been so simple and uncomplicated, and somehow this love was so very different. It seemed so much more intense, and not for the complications that were involved, but more because James seemed to arouse that intenseness in her, a new depth of feeling, one she had never experienced before.

His lovemaking was as deeply arousing as ever, but somehow subtly different. He told her how beautiful she was, how sexy she was, how deeply she excited him. He undressed her, unhurriedly, because that was the way he liked it. His sensual, erotic, exploratory caresses brought her need to breaking-point, so that when he finally entered her the pleasure was all the more intense.

She silently mouthed the words she was too afraid to admit to him—that she loved him so very much. She thought he must know as she gasped in ecstasy as he moved so urgently into her. She thought that she must know that he loved her, because no one made love like this without the ultimate commitment.

But there were no words as their climax broke, just the impassioned gasps of deep, intense pleasure as they clung to each other, trembling with passion in the darkness, as the flames of the fire danced shadows all around them.

CHAPTER NINE

IT WAS the first time James had stayed the night in the cottage, and Fern was the first to awake. His arm was around her waist, in the same position as when they had drifted into sleep the night before. But Fern didn't reflect on last night. Her immediate thought was for Charley, and it powered such tension to her body that she got up so quickly that her head swam.

Shakily she dressed and hurried to his room, but he was still asleep, and when she looked at his bright red alarm clock by the side of his bed she understood why. It was only five-thirty.

Gently she closed the door after her and, instead of going back to bed, went downstairs to make tea. Sacha had taken to sleeping in front of the Aga instead of with Charley, probably because up at Bourne Hall she had got so used to it. The influence of the Hall's household had even filtered down to Charley's pet, Fern thought ruefully.

Sacha stretched and yawned and made little whining sounds in the back of her throat and Fern gave her a biscuit to keep her quiet; she didn't want everyone woken up yet.

She put the kettle on the hob and glanced up at the toby jug on the shelf above the range.

Her fingers were trembling as she took it down. It was dusty, and she blew on it and smoothed her fingers over the colourful glaze. She felt guilty for having neglected the housework recently, allowing the dust to accumulate. Her only excuse was that her life was so full. Her mail order was going well, and then there was Victoria and Charley. If Charley wasn't up at the Hall, Victoria was down at the cottage. James's daughter was growing too fond of her, Fern thought painfully, and she was growing too fond of her. But you couldn't help loving the offspring of the man you loved; it was inevitable.

But was she just feeling guilty because of the dust on Ralph's toby jug? No, not only that. She clutched it to her chest and closed her eyes, and the guilt wouldn't go away—the guilt for loving James more.

'You loved him very much, didn't you?'

Startled, Fern turned to face James. He was standing behind her, fully dressed as she was, and she knew why and understood.

'Yes,' she murmured, lowering her eyes to gaze down at the jug in her hands. Yes, she had, but somehow this new love for James was so much deeper. Her love for Ralph had been without complications, a young love that had travelled a simple, straightforward path to marriage. But the path to James's love was strewn with fears and doubts and complications, and because of the pain she was suffering she knew the love she had for James went beyond anything she had ever felt before.

'Do you feel guilty?' he asked in a low voice.

Fern's gaze shot up to meet his and she was shocked to see how dark and impenetrable his eyes were. He was ahead of her in his assumption of her thoughts, but she was nowhere in trying to read his.

'G-guilty for what?' she asked softly.

'For us, of course. We are lovers, Fern, and you haven't had any since your husband, and that must make for a feeling of confusion and guilt; at least I presume it might.' He sounded as if he wasn't sure about that, but Fern knew what he was getting at.

She nodded and lowered her lashes and knew in that moment that she couldn't tell him the truth about her guilty feelings—that she loved him so much more than she had ever loved before. 'I do feel a guilt; at least I think it's guilt' she admitted. 'But not because I loved him and feel as if I'm betraying his memory, but...well...Charley lives on...'

'And he's an extension of your late husband, and if you are betraying his memory you are betraying Charley?'

Fern turned away and put the jug back on the shelf. 'I don't know,' she murmured.

'But you must know, Fern,' he grated softly, turning her back to face him. 'For both our sakes you must know.'

'W-why?' she asked tremulously. 'It's my problem to cope with, not yours!'

'So you're saying I have no part in your life?' He sounded hurt.

Fern's hopes rose and swam. 'It's not that... It's...'

'It's what, Fern? What are you afraid to admit to?'

He *knew* how she felt about him! He had guessed! Her hopes failed her then. She couldn't tell him, because this was the ultimate fear—the terrible fear of ridicule and rejection—and no matter how hard you tried to think rationally it was still there. Rachel had sown her wicked seeds well; they were in full bloom now, spoiling her love, making it seem hopeless. They were ill-suited...she but a suburban mother... No! Rachel wasn't going to win, not that way!

'And what are you afraid to admit to, James?' she said hoarsely. 'You sounded hurt when you suggested you had no part in my life, as if you cared——'

'I do care, and I'm hurt at the suggestion——'

'But you aren't willing to give any part of yourself. You want me to admit to something that might stroke your ego, but you haven't been honest with me from the start.' She shook her head miserably. 'I don't mean Rachel——'

'So what do you mean, Fern?' he grated, but not softly now. Now he was showing anger, and that bred anger, and Fern was feeling it towards him too, because she was so unsure of everything and he wasn't helping, he just wasn't.

'Your wife, James!' she hit back coldly.

He tensed and a shutter seemed to mist over his eyes, and his hands dropped to his sides.

'I told you—no wife,' he breathed quietly, but though he denied it with cool composure there was a give-away pulse of a nerve at his temple.

The kettle hissed softly and Fern was glad of the reason to turn away from him to slide it off the hob. How could he deny it? Angrily she spun back to him, because she wanted the truth, because they had no future without it. It had always been at the back of her mind, this unknown taboo person who no one knew anything about.

'I wouldn't have considered this affair if she were in evidence, James,' she breathed hotly. 'I've had enough feelings of my own to come to terms with.' She stepped away from him. 'Look at us both, fully dressed at this time of the morning because we are both as guilty as hell at what we are doing—having an affair behind our children's backs. Making love behind locked doors, downstairs on sofas, away from prying eyes——'

'That's the only way at the moment, Fern,' he rasped back at her. 'Dear God, but married couples with children do that all the time, for want of privacy!'

Fern steeled herself. 'I know,' she said stiffly. 'I've been married, don't forget.'

'How can I ever forget? It's there between us all the time, some barrier that you're putting up at every opportunity——'

'I'm not!' Fern protested. 'It . . . it has been a problem for me . . . I'm dealing with it, or trying to. This isn't a normal relationship, a normal affair——'

'So at least you recognise it as one—an affair, as you put it—and no, it isn't the general run-of-the-mill affair. . . God!' He raked a hand through his hair in frustration. 'What is it with that word that jars with me? Fern, this is a *love*-affair, not just a bloody commonplace affair!'

Love! Fern's heart jerked perilously at the word. Every pulse raced to the surface of her skin. But this wasn't how she wanted it. Yes, she was desperate to hear those words, but having them thrown in the midst of an argument wasn't the way she wanted to hear them. She steeled her heart at what she wanted to believe, because still he couldn't be honest with her.

'Now you're using my marriage as a barrier, to deflect away from your own,' she told him quietly. 'You want me to bring my feelings out into the open, but how can I . . . ? How can I admit——?'

'That you love me?' he rasped.

Her hand came up to her mouth to repress a small cry, and then she turned away to fumble with cups and tea and sugar.

He swung her back to him. 'Quit that cosy domestic act and concentrate on me, which is far more important at the moment. Is it so very hard to say, Fern, or am I wrong? Have I been deceiving myself?'

Fern fell into such a long silence that she felt his grip tighten on her shoulders, as if he was going to shake the very truth out of her limp body. She swallowed, determined not to give in, because it would hurt so very much. *This* love hurt so very much, more than she had ever endured in her life before. Slowly she raised her eyes to his; they were raw and misted with tears, and she had to struggle hard to fight them back.

'You have no right to ask such a thing of me, James, when you are so reluctant to give anything yourself. You say, "No wife", as if... as if it isn't a problem——'

'And it isn't.'

'But it damned well is!' Fern insisted. 'You claim not to be a widower, not to be a divorcee... well, Victoria was begotten in some sort of relationship!' She pulled away from him, then stepped back and looked directly into his eyes. 'I won't admit to loving you because I can't love someone who isn't honest——'

'I've never lied to you,' he said darkly.

'That's not the same as being honest!'

They glared at each other and then James sagged his shoulders so wearily that it tore at Fern's heart. Oh, God, what was he trying to hold back from her? Why, oh, why was he holding back?

'Can't you accept that there is no wife in my life? Isn't it enough for you that I spend every minute I can with you? Doesn't that mean anything to you at all?'

There was a movement upstairs and Fern stared in dismay at James. His shoulders tensed again. At least his eyes didn't shift guiltily from hers, but they were different now, cold and impenetrable.

Sacha heard the movement, rushed across the kitchen, and bounded up the stairs. It broke the eye contact between them, and James stiffly picked up his jacket from the back of the chair.

'For the record,' he said after he'd slipped it on and plunged his hands deep into the pockets. 'Not that it will make any difference to your feelings for me, which in my opinion are wafer-thin anyway, but I'm not married and never have been.'

Fern almost reeled with the shock of that. Her heart constricted so wildly that she understood what a heart attack must feel like. The breath went from her lungs and she opened her mouth to speak, but nothing happened.

'Surprised?' he grated sardonically, and when she didn't answer he went on brutally. 'If I thought this "affair" meant anything to you I'd tell you why, but it's quite apparent that your only concern is that your son doesn't see you in bed with a lover. Well, he won't, I assure you; not this lover, anyway.'

He turned, just once, at the porch door on his way out, his face white and impassive as he spoke. 'Now you know something that not even my daughter knows, and, as you're a caring mother yourself, I trust you not to speak of it to anyone.'

The slam of the door after him was like the slamming of the door on his heart.

'Sacha's gone!' Charley cried as he tore into Fern's studio.

Fern hated working when Charley came home from school, but this so-called cottage industry was fast becoming big business. She was flooded with orders and even if she weren't she would have made work for herself. Anything to rid herself of that terrible confession of James's which she was trying so hard to understand and come to terms with.

'She'll be back, don't worry,' Fern soothed absently. 'She's probably chasing rabbits in the meadow.'

'She isn't!' Charley persisted. 'I've looked and called and she *won't* come. I know where she is and I'm going to get her!'

'Charley, no!' Fern cried, rushing after him and catching him as he was about to open the front door.

'She's probably not there.' She knew what was going through her son's mind. Any excuse to get up to the Hall.

Fern found she was shaking as she held her son firmly by the shoulders. 'We...we'll go and look in the meadow——'

'She's not there,' Charley whined. 'I told you she's not there. You don't listen to me!' He stamped his foot, and Fern saw shades of Victoria's behaviour coming out in her own son. 'Why can't I go up to get Sacha? We haven't been for ages——'

'Three days, Charley, not ages, and you must realise that I have work to do and so does everyone else. The world doesn't revolve around you and Victoria, you know. Sacha might not be there, anyway.'

'She is, I *know* she is! She loves it there and so do I and... and you won't let us go!' He burst into tears, tore out of Fern's arms, and rushed upstairs, slamming his bedroom door after him.

Fern stood trembling by the front door. Her hands came up and dragged her hair from her forehead. Oh, God, this was awful. She had hated making excuses to Charley and refusing Sara's suggestion to go back with them to the Hall after school each day. If Sara suspected anything was wrong she hadn't said. Fern had covered herself well, saying she had so much work to do that she just didn't have the time.

Three days wasn't a problem, but how much longer could she keep it up? Already Charley was getting irritable withdrawal symptoms at not seeing Victoria so frequently; apparently school hours were not enough. He talked constantly of the lambs as well, which made Fern feel ten times worse for what she was doing— avoiding James Causton.

She could do no right, she thought miserably as she picked up the phone. She had been in the wrong when James had stormed out; she should have gone after him or at least tried to get in touch with him to say she was sorry. And she was sorry, desperately sorry for not having greater faith in him. She had forced out of him something he had not been ready to tell her—that... that Victoria was illegitimate. It would have come in time, she felt sure, because you couldn't keep that to yourself if you had a future with someone.

Fern hesitated, her shaky fingers trailing over the dial of the phone. But perhaps James had never anticipated a future with her and that was why he hadn't told her before. He had only confessed in anger anyway. Oh, hell, she didn't know anything any more, only that Sacha was missing and that was the immediate problem and nothing else should matter.

She hoped Sara would answer, but just as James did she remembered it was Sara's night off and she was going out with Tim, her own brother. How damned ironic all this was.

'James, it's Fern.' Her heart raced as she said it, and she hurriedly added in case he thought this was a social call, 'Sacha is missing. I don't suppose—— Good grief, what's that noise?'

'Victoria,' James imparted wearily. 'Throwing a tantrum, lying on the floor kicking her heels as if she were two years old again.'

Fern couldn't even smile at that; she knew the feeling too well. Her eyes flicked up to the ceiling where Charley was above, thumping around his room in a temper.

'Charley's quite worried about Sacha,' she went on. 'Have you seen her at all?'

'No, I haven't,' James said coolly, 'but I suppose it's in my interests to go out and take a look around.' He sounded as if that was the last thing on earth he wanted to do, but he had his precious lambs to think about, Fern supposed. 'She's not in season, is she?' he added as an afterthought.

'Heavens, no. Why?'

'Thought she might be out looking for a mate.'

'I thought it was usually the other way round—the males coming to seek the females out.'

There was a very small silence before he said, 'Yes, of course; true to human life too, some might think.'

Fern wondered if that was a hint that it was up to her to make some approach to him! It jarred her conscience for a second. He had a point, cryptic though it was. She opened her mouth to try and make some sort of amends, though it was hardly the time, but he spoke before she had a chance to form any sort of conciliatory words.

'I'll call you if she's around.' The line went dead.

'Don't put yourself out!' Fern muttered as she slammed the phone down.

'Charley!' she called as she pulled on her jacket. She looked out of the small hall window. It would be getting dark in about an hour and if they didn't find Sasha quickly she could be out for the night. There was little left of the snow after a mild spell, but now the weather was chilly again. 'Charley, get your coat; we're going out to look for Sacha.'

Fifteen minutes later, as they tramped back up the lane without a sighting of Sacha, Fern was beginning to think this was not such a smart idea. No one was in the cottage if James phoned to say Sacha was up at Bourne Hall, and it was most likely that she was.

'If we go across the meadow now we might find her,' Charley suggested, pulling at Fern's sleeve.

It was possible Sacha was burrowing at some rabbit hole at the hedgerows—there were enough of them around—but the other side of the meadow finished close to Bourne Hall, and Charley would insist on looking in the stables and the barns. Fern sighed in resignation and headed for the meadow. Better that they found Sacha than James finding her and bringing her home. Fern wouldn't be able to face him in her own home after the last painfully fraught time.

'Mummy, what's that?' Charley cried.

'Shush.' They both listened, and the sound was unmistakable. A small, fretful whimpering sound. They both broke into a run.

Charley saw his dog first and with a terrible cry of anguish flung himself at the hedgerow. Sacha lay beneath it, whimpering pitifully, her tail thumping pathetically on dry leaves at sight of them. One of her back legs was tangled in rusty barbed wire, so badly tangled that she couldn't move.

Fern dropped to her knees. Oh, God, there was blood everywhere. She could see that Sacha had struggled and made it so much worse. Charley was sobbing hysterically.

'Charley, listen to me, darling.' She took his shoulders firmly but gently, willing him to stop crying. 'Get James. I can't move her without help. There . . . there's a gate.' She nodded her head to further down the meadow.

Charley suddenly cried out and stumbled towards James and Victoria, who were heading their way, breaking into a run at the sight of the distressed boy.

'Oh, thank God!' Fern breathed. She was holding Sacha's head as James dropped down beside her.

'Get back!' he shouted at the children as they crowded in, Victoria wailing now at the sight of Sacha struggling so weakly and helplessly.

Tenderly Fern eased her hands out from under the dog's head and scrambled up to grab hold of the children to keep them out of the way. They both clung to her, burying their heads in her jacket and sobbing as James tore at the other end of the barbed wire to free it from the hedgerow.

'Fern, take the children back to the house,' James said quietly. 'Call the vet—the number's on the pad by the kitchen phone. Tell him what's happened and that I'm bringing her down in the Land Rover.' He looked up at her, and his eyes were so desperately unhopeful that Fern stemmed a cry of anguish in her throat.

The two children were still clinging to her, one at each side, half their faces pressed fearfully against her, not bearing to look at Sacha's distress. Suddenly Fern clamped her gloved hands over their free ears.

'Is it bad?' she whispered.

James met her eyes and nodded. 'I can't get the wire out,' he whispered back. 'It's half embedded in her foot and it looks as if she's torn an artery. She's losing quite a bit of blood. I'll have to hurry.' He turned his attention back to Sacha, and, sure that the other end of the wire was free of the hedge, he lifted the heavy, whimpering dog up into his arms.

'You go ahead,' he huffed, 'and tell the vet what I've just told you.'

Fern nodded and, grabbing the children's hands, she hurried to the gate that led to the house. The children ran with her, silent now, recognising the urgency.

There was no one in the warm kitchen and Fern dashed straight to the phone and snatched it up. Victoria was at her side, thrusting the pad into her hands. The child was trembling and her face was white and tear-streaked.

'You and Charley take your coats and boots off,' Fern urged, not wanting them to hear what she was saying. Both children obeyed instantly, sitting on the floor by the back door to take off their boots.

Fern made the call quickly and efficiently. 'Yes, golden Labrador, female...' She heard the Land Rover speeding away outside, urgently grazing on the gravel. 'Look, could you tell Mr Causton to phone here as soon as the vet has seen Sacha? Yes, thank you very much.' With trembling hands she hooked the receiver back on to the wall.

'Is...is Sacha going to die?' Victoria whispered at her side, her tiny hand slipping into Fern's.

'N...no,' Fern husked and squeezed the little hand reassuringly. 'She's...she's too precious to die.'

Solemnly Victoria turned to Charley, who stood quiet and pale-faced by the mound of boots at the back door. Victoria took his hand and led him to the rug in front of the Aga, the rug Sacha always stretched out on when she was here. Without a word being spoken, the two children dropped on their knees and lowered their heads and squeezed tight their eyes.

'Dear God,' Victoria started, 'please save Sacha...'

Fern turned away, not able to bear it. She covered her face with her hands and silently cried.

The children wouldn't settle. Fern made cups of milky cocoa and tried to get them interested in games and books, but one or other of them kept darting to the kitchen door to listen for the Land Rover, though Fern had told them umpteen times that the phone call would come first.

It was dark now and the house made strange creaking sounds.

'Where's Annie?' Fern asked, wishing she were here to add some support.

'At her sister's, and Sara is out with Uncle Tim,' Victoria told her.

Fern smiled; it seemed that Tim was Victoria's uncle now.

They all jumped when the phone rang, and Fern snatched at it.

'Oh, James,' she breathed with relief at last. 'Thank goodness...'

Charley and Victoria shouted out excitedly, and Fern had to shush them to hear what James was saying. 'Tomorrow? Wonderful...' She listened. 'Good...great... James...? Hurry home,' she added softly.

'Is she all right? Is she?'

'She's fine,' Fern told them, hugging them to her. 'The vet got the piece of wire out of her foot and had to stitch up an artery——'

'What's an artery?' Victoria asked, and Charley gave her a shove.

'Oh, something,' Fern breathed evasively. 'Anyway, she's all right, but the vet wants to keep her overnight——'

'Oh, no!' was the chorus.

'Oh, yes.' Fern grinned. 'She's had an anaesthetic——'

'What's an an...ana——'

Charley pushed at Victoria again. 'You can't even say it!'

'You say it, then!' Victoria dared.

'Anaesthetic,' Charley said perfectly and not without smugness.

Victoria's mouth dropped open with surprise and a sudden new respect.

'Anyway,' Fern butted in, 'she'll be home tomorrow and she'll need lots of loving *and* lots of peace and quiet, so be warned.'

It was another hour before James returned, and at the first sound of tyres on gravel the two children were out of the back door at the speed of light.

Fern hung back; suddenly the weight of the whole evening dragged her down. The anguish of finding Sacha that way and the children's distress had been bad enough to cope with, and now everything was all right, except it wasn't all right with her and James, and now she desperately wanted it to be.

Later, when all the fuss about Sacha had died down, she would tell him how stupid and blind and unreasonable she had been, and more than anything she would tell him she loved him, because she hadn't yet and it had been a grave omission on her part.

When James walked into the kitchen with two children scooped up into his arms Fern felt weak with her feelings for him. Their eyes met for an instant but then two wriggling, inquisitive children took over his attention, demanding lurid details, demanding to know when their dear Sacha would be back with them. Quietly and unobtrusively Fern tidied up the books and games on the refectory table and waited patiently for her turn to come.

It didn't till much later that evening when the children were settled in bed. Nothing had been said about Charley staying the night; it had just been silently accepted that he would. Fern wondered if that went for her too.

'How's your hand?' she asked as James poured them drinks in the sitting-room. Fern sat on the edge of her armchair, warming her hands at the log fire. She had lit it earlier, part of her plan to make everything right between her and James.

'Just a scratch from the barbed wire,' he told her as he handed her a large gin and tonic with his bandaged hand. He smiled down at her. 'The vet dealt with it, or rather his veterinary nurse did.'

'A bit of a blow to your pride, that——' Fern smiled ruefully '—having your wounds attended to by a veterinary nurse.'

'The tetanus booster in my backside was more of a blow to my ego.' He grinned and added, 'But she was a very pretty nurse.'

Fern put down her glass and in a second she had thrown herself into his arms, locking her arms around his neck as if never to be parted from him, and she wouldn't be, not ever.

'Oh, James Causton, I love you; I love you so very much. I hate myself but I love you!'

Slowly his arms came around her, and she felt a shudder of relief spasm through him. Gently he held her against him, breathing quietly into her hair.

'You mustn't hate yourself; you have nothing to hate yourself for,' he murmured, nuzzling her hair.

'But I have, James.' She drew back from him to look into his wonderful face, which was drawn with fatigue after the anguish he'd suffered for Sacha. 'A-about your wife... I forced that out of you when I should have waited. I was so confused and worried about us that I thought she was the reason...' She shook her head. 'But no, that was only part of it... It was more my own insecurity... I didn't think you loved me...'

'I do love you, Fern, desperately so. I thought you must know that,' he told her earnestly.

'I should have...I know I should have...but there was so much to consider—the children, and...you knew everything about me, about Ralph, and...and I knew nothing about you. I thought that you were separated...and then I wasn't sure.' She bit her lip and looked deep into his eyes. 'You know, since you told me you were never married I've tried to understand what you've been through. I...I suppose she—Victoria's mother—left you with the child, and that must have been hard, and then bringing up your daughter...'

Suddenly his hands dropped to his sides and he tried to turn away, but Fern held him.

'James, these days it doesn't matter if a child is born outside marriage——'

'Fern, you don't understand. It's more than that, much more than that.' His hands came up and smoothed down her cheeks, and he smiled at her, and then suddenly his face was so relaxed. It was as if he had come to a decision, and making it had driven the anguish out of him. 'I couldn't be honest with you from the start, Fern——'

'You couldn't trust me?' Fern burned with the thought of that.

His hands dropped to her shoulders again, his fingers splaying out to caress over her tension. 'How could I? I didn't know where any of this was going. I wanted you from the very first moment I saw you, out in that meadow, giving me hell for locking your dog up for the night. That need turned very quickly to love, but I wasn't sure about you and I had to be sure that you really cared before I could put my trust in you.'

The tension wouldn't go away; it was taut through her body, and the doubt showed in her eyes.

'Don't look at me like that, Fern; my only wrong has been in not having more faith in you. You never said how you felt about me. If you've had doubts, so have I.' His thumb brushed her chin. 'I wanted so much for you to admit your love for me the other morning down at the cottage——'

'I...I couldn't, and then I thought that you must know, and I was so afraid of rejection, and then you got angry with me for probing about your wife. Oh, James, I'm sorry, truly sorry, but I still can't understand why you weren't completely honest with me be-fore——'

'And I still haven't been,' he interrupted gravely.

Fern frowned up at him. 'What...what do you mean?' she breathed quickly.

He took her hands and urged her to sit next to him on the sofa. He held on to her hands, smoothing his fingers over hers and gazing down at them. All the time Fern held her breath, her heart hammering under her ribcage. There was more, and he was afraid to tell her. She wanted to help him, but didn't know how; but she must try.

'James,' she breathed quietly, 'I love Victoria too. I couldn't help but love her, feeling the way I do for you. She's your beautiful daughter and I love her, and, whatever is troubling you, I'm with you all the way.'

He looked at her then, his eyes brimming with his love for her. 'I'm glad you said that, Fern, my darling,' he whispered. 'It makes it easier for me.' He took a ragged breath, but still the words wouldn't come, and she twisted her hands under his till she was gripping him fiercely, urging him on. 'Fern... Victoria...she's not my daughter.'

Fern's heart spun with shock, so painfully that she thought she would pass out. Her head swam dizzily. She gasped, because she didn't understand.

'But I love her as deeply as if she were my own,' he went on quickly. 'I adopted her when she was nine months old and so therefore I am her father, but not in the true sense.'

'But...but...how...? I don't understand,' Fern breathed, the words coming in a rush of confused heat.

He looked down at her hands again, as if it was too painful to face her.

'She's my brother's child,' he uttered quietly. 'My own beloved niece.' He took another deep breath. 'She was conceived in a happy marriage—my brother's and Eva's, his wife. They had a farm down in Dorset. Their life was good; they worshipped each other and Victoria was much wanted and loved deeply. Then one night they were out celebrating a wedding anniversary, driving home...rushing home to their baby...' His voice cracked and Fern instinctively tightened her grip on him. 'They were hit by a drunken driver——'

'Oh, God!' Fern moaned, and her head dropped down and she closed her eyes with agonised shock.

'Eva died instantly... My brother lived for six hours. We were close... I was with him when he died. He made me promise to look after Victoria, but I didn't need to make such a promise. I would have done it willingly anyway.'

Fern sobbed, flung her arms around his neck, and clung to him. James held her strongly, only slightly trembling against her as she cried.

'Oh, James,' she cried. 'I love you so much, more than ever for that if it's possible.' She drew back from him, the tears streaming down her face, her eyes wide and glazed with the thoughts of the horrors he must have felt at losing his brother, and through that grief he had cared so lovingly for his baby niece. 'Victoria,' she breathed raggedly. 'Does she...does she know?'

He shook his head. 'She doesn't know that I'm not her real father, but of course she's always known she has no mother. She was only a baby when it happened, so she had no recall. She hasn't been an easy child and there have been difficulties, and the time to tell her has never been right. Her grandparents—Eva's parents—were devastated at losing their only daughter, so much so that they couldn't cope. It was all too much for them. Willingly they let me take over Victoria's welfare. They adored my brother too. They weren't young grandparents and the strain of such a small baby would have been beyond them. They agreed I should look after her. I had everything to give her, everything money could buy and more. They have always been an important part of her life and together we decided to wait till she was older before telling her. One day she will have to be told . . . one day.'

Fern wiped a tear from her face and fought back the rest that were pressing for release. Without hesitation she lifted her hands and held James's face.

'And I'll be with you when you do,' she told him strongly. 'It will be easy, so easy, my darling.'

He looked puzzled, and she smiled and then gave a small laugh. 'She's surrounded by love, James, and that is the most important thing in a child's life.' Her face was flushed with the faith of that statement. She laughed again, to ease the terrible strain of all that he had told her. 'It will be all right, darling. You know Victoria; she hates little Charley to get one over on her.'

'What do you mean?'

'I mean that when you and I are married you are going to have to adopt another child.' She kissed his lips then, tenderly, lovingly, promisingly. 'You're going to have to adopt Charley if you want him to carry your name, and then maybe that might be the time to tell Victoria, just so that she feels she's equal to him.' She frowned suddenly and shook her head. 'But maybe that wouldn't be the right time.' Her face broke into a warm smile. 'We'll find the right time, James; together we'll know when it comes and when it's the right moment ... And another thing ...' Her eyes danced mischievously. 'I don't know the system, but *I* might have to adopt Victoria myself to be her proper mother.'

James laughed and pulled her hard into his arms, and brushed a kiss across her lips before saying, 'Darling, haven't you forgotten one small but very relevant point?'

'Oh?' she murmured quizzically. 'I thought I'd got it all wrapped up.'

'You have, almost ...' He paused, and his dark eyes were glittering with humour. 'But you've forgotten one thing that is very important—in fact essential—to your plans. I haven't asked you to marry me yet.'

A hot tide of embarrassment rushed over Fern and then she smiled sheepishly. 'But...but you...you will...'

He looked doubtful and then lowered his mouth to hers, and she clung to him and knew.

Her arms encircled him and she mouthed kisses across his face and chin, and when he responded with the heat of his love she pulled back from him.

'James,' she said sternly, 'you still haven't said it.'

He tipped her chin and looked straight into her eyes. 'Marry me, my darling Fern, because I love and need you and ... and ...' His eyes danced ' ...I think I might be losing Sara, and that's all your fault.'

'So you *do* want my cosy domesticity after all!' she laughed.

He gathered her back into his arms and murmured, 'That's not exactly what I want at the moment.'

His lips on hers told her *exactly* what he wanted and her own echoed his desire, and as his hand slid under her sweater to smooth over the silken skin Fern wondered what the children would say in the morning when they told them there were going to be a few changes in the household in the near future.

'What are you thinking?' James murmured as he shifted their position on the sofa so he could undress her properly.

'Nothing,' she murmured softly. This wasn't a time to be thinking of children and dogs and nannies and uncles. She slid her hands under his sweater to feel the strength of his back, to run her hands down his warm, hard flesh, to loosen the top of his cord jeans. 'Only that I love you very much and isn't it wonderful that we don't have to worry about locked doors and making love on sofas any more?'

As he cupped her breast and lowered his mouth to graze his tongue hungrily over the heated tip he murmured, 'That's what you think.'

But Fern didn't hear, because love was rushing her senses, swirling in her ears. This new, deep, deep love was hers and James's, uniquely theirs, a love that was like no other.

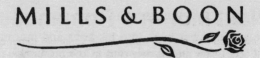

MILLS & BOON

Forthcoming Titles

DUET
Available in February

The Carole Mortimer Duet **ELUSIVE AS THE UNICORN**
MEMORIES OF THE PAST

The Susan Napier Duet **TRUE ENCHANTER**
FORTUNE'S MISTRESS

FAVOURITES
Available in March

A BITTER HOMECOMING Robyn Donald
DARK PURSUIT Charlotte Lamb

LOVE ON CALL
Available in March

NO MORE SECRETS Lilian Darcy
TILL SUMMER ENDS Hazel Fisher
TAKE A DEEP BREATH Margaret O'Neill
HEALING LOVE Meredith Webber

Available from W.H. Smith, John Menzies, Volume One,
Forbuoys, Martins, Tesco, Asda, Safeway and other paperback
stockists.

Also available from Mills & Boon Reader Service,
Freepost, P.O. Box 236, Croydon, Surrey CR9 9EL.

Readers in South Africa - write to:
Book Services International Ltd, P.O. Box 41654,
Craighall, Transvaal 2024.

Next Month's Romances

Each month you can choose from a wide variety of romance with Mills & Boon. Below are the new titles to look out for next month, why not ask either Mills & Boon Reader Service or your Newsagent to reserve you a copy of the titles you want to buy – just tick the titles you would like and either post to Reader Service or take it to any Newsagent and ask them to order your books.

Please save me the following titles: Please tick   ✓

HEART OF THE OUTBACK	Emma Darcy	
DARK FIRE	Robyn Donald	
SEPARATE ROOMS	Diana Hamilton	
GUILTY LOVE	Charlotte Lamb	
GAMBLE ON PASSION	Jacqueline Baird	
LAIR OF THE DRAGON	Catherine George	
SCENT OF BETRAYAL	Kathryn Ross	
A LOVE UNTAMED	Karen van der Zee	
TRIUMPH OF THE DAWN	Sophie Weston	
THE DARK EDGE OF LOVE	Sara Wood	
A PERFECT ARRANGEMENT	Kay Gregory	
RELUCTANT ENCHANTRESS	Lucy Keane	
DEVIL'S QUEST	Joanna Neil	
UNWILLING SURRENDER	Cathy Williams	
ALMOST AN ANGEL	Debbie Macomber	
THE MARRIAGE BRACELET	Rebecca Winters	

If you would like to order these books in addition to your regular subscription from Mills & Boon Reader Service please send £1.90 per title to: Mills & Boon Reader Service, Freepost, P.O. Box 236, Croydon, Surrey, CR9 9EL, quote your Subscriber No:.................................... (If applicable) and complete the name and address details below. Alternatively, these books are available from many local Newsagents including W.H.Smith, J.Menzies, Martins and other paperback stockists from 12 March 1994.

Name:...

Address:...

....Post Code:........................

To Retailer: If you would like to stock M&B books please contact your regular book/magazine wholesaler for details.

You may be mailed with offers from other reputable companies as a result of this application.
If you would rather not take advantage of these opportunities please tick box   ☐

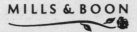

FREE BOOK OFFER

HEARTS OF FIRE

By Miranda Lee

HEARTS OF FIRE by Miranda Lee is a totally compelling six-part saga set in Australia's glamorous but cut-throat world of gem dealing.

Discover the passion, scandal, sin and finally the hope that exist between two fabulously rich families. You'll be hooked from the very first page as Gemma Smith fights for the secret of the priceless **Heart of Fire** black opal and fights for love too...

Each novel features a gripping romance in itself. And **SEDUCTION AND SACRIFICE,** the first title in this exciting series, is due for publication in April but you can order your FREE copy, worth £2.50, NOW! To receive your FREE book simply complete the coupon below and return it to:

**MILLS & BOON READER SERVICE, FREEPOST,
P.O. BOX 236, CROYDON CR9 9EL.   TEL: 081-684 2141**

NO STAMP NEEDED

Ms/Mrs/Miss/Mr: _____   HOF

Address _____

_____

_____ Postcode

mps MAILING PREFERENCE SERVICE